A quick circuit of the room showed nothing, confirming what I already knew: it was empty, the intruder gone. I let out a sigh. Nothing like a pile of problems to make life interesting.

Then something fluttered to my left. I turned to get a closer look. The curtain had been shredded and was covered in long black hair. I recognized it immediately. It belonged to a very large and very determined were-wolf.

Damn it all to hell and back.

I lowered my blade and felt the itch in my spine a split second too late as a hairy set of claw-tipped hands wrapped themselves around my throat. I let out a strangled squawk, my hands first going for the claws, and then stopping to lower my blade.

I couldn't use it, not on this one.

PRAISE FOR SHANNON MAYER AND THE RYLEE ADAMSON SERIES

"If you love the early Anita Blake novels by Laurel K. Hamilton, you will fall head over heels for The Rylee Adamson Series. Rylee is a complex character with a tough, kick-ass exterior, a sassy temperament, and morals which she never deviates from. She's the ultimate heroine. Mayer's books rank right up there with Kim Harrison's, Patricia Brigg's, and Ilona Andrew's. Get ready for a whole new take on Urban Fantasy and Paranormal Romance and be ready to be glued to the pages!"

—*Just My Opinion Book Blog*

"Rylee is the perfect combination of loyal, intelligent, compassionate, and kick-ass. Many times, the heroines in urban fantasy novels tend to be so tough or snarky that they come off as unlikable. Rylee is a smart-ass for sure, but she isn't insulting. Well, I guess the she gets a little sassy with the bad guys, but then it's just hilarious."

—*Diary of a Bibliophile*

"I could not put it down. Not only that, but I immediately started the next book in the series, *Immune*."

—*Just Talking Books*

"*Priceless* was one of those reads that just starts off running and doesn't give too much time to breathe. . . . I'll just go ahead and add the rest of the books to my TBR list now."

—*Vampire Book Club*

"This book is so great and it blindsided me. I'm always looking for something to tide me over until the next Ilona Andrews or Patricia Briggs book comes out, but no matter how many recommendations I get nothing ever measures up. This was as close as I've gotten and I'm so freakin happy!"

—*Dynamite Review*

PRICELESS

Books by Shannon Mayer

PRICELESS

A RYLEE ADAMSON NOVEL
BOOK 1

SHANNON MAYER

TALOS
New York

First Talos Press edition published 2016

Talos Press books may be purchased in bulk at special discounts for
sales promotion, corporate gifts, fund-raising, or educational purposes.
Special editions can also be created to specifications. For details, contact
the Special Sales Department, Talos Press, 307 West 36th Street, 11th
Floor, New York, NY 10018 or info@skyhorsepublishing.com.

Talos Press® is a registered trademark of Skyhorse Publishing, Inc.®,
a Delaware corporation.

Visit our website at www.talospress.com.

10 9 8 7 6 5 4 3 2 1

Library of Congress Cataloging-in-Publication Data is available on file.

Original illustrations by Damon Za www.damonza.com

Print ISBN: 978-1-940456-95-9

Printed in Canada

ACKNOWLEDGEMENTS

Priceless has been sitting on my "To do" shelf for a LONG time. Several years in fact. I had the chance to read the first scene to my writers group and got some great feedback, enough that I thought, "Yes, I will finish this story!"

So a great "huzzah" to my writers group, WIP (aka Writing In Progress), who without I might not have settled down to finish Rylee's story or have realized that she was a character I couldn't wait to know more about.

Of course, I would be remiss if I didn't thank my editors, Melissa Breau and NL "Jinxie" Gervasio, who both worked hard to help me bring *Priceless* forward.

Not to mention my readers! You are AMAZING and have been so supportive with your reviews (which I love reading!) your words of encouragement on my Fan Page and your heartfelt emails. *Hugs* to you all!

Finally, to my main squeeze, my husband and best friend. You never read my books, you don't really understand fantasy, horror, or romance as it pertains to reading, but you cheer me on anyway.

Thank you for loving me, encouraging me, and making me laugh.

CAST OF CHARACTERS

Rylee Adamson: Tracker and Immune
Liam O'Shea: FBI agent
Giselle: Mentored Rylee and Milly
Millicent: AKA Milly; Witch who is best friend to Rylee
John: Motel owner; friend of Rylee
Mary: Wife of John
India: A spirit seeker
Martins: O'Shea's FBI partner
Kyle Jacobs: Rylee's personal hacker
Doran: Daywalker and Shaman
Alex: A werewolf and friend of Rylee's
Berget: Rylee's little sister
Dox: Large pale blue-skinned ogre; Friend of Rylee
Maria: Mother of missing child
Don: Father of missing child
Louisa: Shaman
Eve: Harpy
Agent Valley: Senior in command in the Arcane Division of the FBI.

1

The couple in front of me looked like any other parents who'd lost a child—their hands gripping one another, dark circles under their eyes, skin sallow from not enough food, water, or sleep—except for the faintest glimmer of a possibility, a scrap of hope that someone had thrown them, by sending them my way. That was the only difference. A difference they were banking on. Every parent's worst nightmare is the reason I have become the best at what I do. Or maybe more accurately, the *only* reason I do what I do.

"Please, the police, they say there is nothing; that they can't help us. They say she's gone, and there are no clues, and they just can't find her. Please, we were told you could help." Maria, the mother, pleaded with me, her whole body begging for me to do what no one else would even dare offer her hope for. Her voice was cultured, upper crust and very East Coast snob. But right now she didn't look it. Clothes rumpled, designer but not pressed or even that clean, hair in disarray, and bags under her eyes. A very childish part of me took pleasure in seeing the mighty brought low. I only wished it wasn't because her kid had been snatched.

I didn't answer her right away, though I had already decided to help them. Her fear and hope filled the room with a tangible weight that choked me, kept me from saying a single word. I wouldn't leave a child out there if I could find her, not even if the kid's parents were wankers. Which, looking at the child's father as he puffed up and prepared to verbally assault me, was obviously the case. I guessed he was a lawyer, or maybe a judge.

"Damn you!" He shot to his feet. His clothes hung off his frame like he was wearing his older brother's hand-me-downs; his fists vibrated at his sides. "Why did you make us come all the way here if you're not even going to try and help? To the middle of North Dakota of all places, to what, tell us 'Oops, sorry, not going to happen?' What kind of sadistic bitch are you?"

I let him—Don, I think his name was—continue his tirade stalking around the cheap hotel room, but didn't interrupt him. No point. He would talk until finally the silence would catch him and smother his words. Maria sat in an overstuffed chair, body all aquiver; her husband's anger a physical energy that obviously upset her. It rolled off me, which only energized him further, gave him more fuel for his wild temper tantrum. The only parents' anger that ever bothered me was my own, and they were both gone from my life. Of course, it had been their decision, forcing me out of their lives when I was sixteen. But what can you expect when I, their adopted child, was accused of killing their biological daughter?

I waited, and another minute passed before he ran out of steam and stood blowing like a spent beast pushed too hard, too fast.

"Are you quite finished, Don?" My voice was low, calm.

He nodded once, a sharp movement that in another circumstance would have me reaching for one of my blades, if I'd had them on me.

I motioned to the couch. "Sit next to your wife. Speak when spoken to, answer my questions, and other than that, shut the hell up." He sat and I gave myself a mental pat on the back.

Good job, Rylee, for a moment there you almost sounded like a grown up in control of a situation.

My vision of him as a lawyer dried up when he didn't even bother to argue. Old money then, working for Daddy's company all his life was my next best guess.

I looked down at the pictures on the cheap hotel coffee table. A little girl smiled up at me; seven years old or there about, with deep auburn hair, not so unlike my own, and hazel eyes—quite different from my own tri-colored ones. Each picture held a different pose, a different place. The park, Christmas sittings, dinner parties. And each picture held a small, seemingly insignificant blush of light, close to the girl.

"What's her name?" My first question of the entire meeting was met with silence. I glanced up only to see Maria close her eyes and tears trickle down her cheeks. Don met my gaze; his hazel eyes the perfect mirror image of his daughter's.

"India." His voice choked over the syllables. They knew, like all my potential clients knew, that if I asked for the child's name, I was in; there was no turning back.

I held another picture up. The same hair and eyes as the first, the face was a little thinner. A year or two older than the previous picture. And the same strange light, this time a little brighter.

"How long has she been missing now?"

Don answered. "Six months tomorrow. Whoever took her did it right under our noses. We were at Deerborn Park, just as the sun was setting."

His words struck me through the heart. The same park my little sister had been stolen from. "Six months, that would make it April?" I clamped down on my emotions. It wouldn't be the same day, no, it wouldn't be . . .

"Yes, the first."

My world spun out from under my feet and it took everything I had to hold it together. I'd run as far away as I could to escape that place and those memories. Yet here I was, facing a child stolen on the same day, from the same park. In my world, there was no such thing as a coincidence. Not of this magnitude.

Don leaned toward me, eyes wide to hold back his tears. I'd seen the move more than once; fathers were always reluctant to let me see them cry. "What are the chances she's already—" He choked up.

I stared at the two pictures for a long second before answering, feeling for India with a talent only I had, an ability that set me apart. No matter where a child was taken, no matter how far or how hidden, I could find them. The brush of her emotions against the inside of my skull were all it took to know she was alive.

"She's still alive. I can tell you that much. But finding her will depend on a lot of factors." What I didn't tell them was how close their daughter was to breaking; her inner shields, which kept her from being controlled, were thin and weakening fast. Not a good sign. I also withheld that I couldn't pinpoint her, which meant she was on the other side of the Veil, another very bad thing. There were hundreds of entrances and not necessarily all connected. I was going to need some help on this one. I stamped down my own memories and emotions, did my best to ignore the similarities between India's case and my sister's.

Maria frowned, a perfect line creasing her brow. "We went to a psychic, but she said India was beyond our reach . . . we assumed that meant—"

I cut her off with the wave of a hand. "Most psychics are frauds. The real deals don't advertise their services."

It was Don's turn to frown. "Is that what you are? A psychic?"

"No." I shook my head and didn't give him anything else. I wasn't sure how much truth these two could handle in such a short period of time.

I scooped up the two pictures, placed them into an envelope, and tucked that into my jacket pocket.

"I don't know how long it will take. There are to be no phone calls, private investigators, or drive-bys. Don't involve the police anymore; if you do, I don't know that I'll be able to get her back for you. Do you understand?" I looked from one to the other. They both nodded.

Maria's eyes were still closed tight, her hands clasped in front of her, her lips moving soundlessly. Praying, most likely. Most parents, even the non-believers, prayed for their missing children to be returned. I could still see my parents praying for Berget, though they'd never stepped foot in a church. The couch creaked as I stood. "Anything else I should know about India before I go? Even the insignificant could be important."

I wanted them to tell me what I'd already guessed. Wanted for them to come clean. But already they were withdrawing, the guilt of hiding what might help showing, they were too afraid to say out loud what was written all over their drawn and haggard faces. I pressed my lips together and started out of the room toward the front entrance, my boots clacking on the cheap linoleum.

"Wait." Maria's voice and the shuffling of papers called me back. I paused and glanced over my shoulder. Maria stood, her clothes hanging off her petite frame, her hands clenching a stack of paper.

"Don't! She doesn't need to see those." Don appeared in the doorway and reached for the rumpled stack.

"And if we don't, and she can't find India, what then? Do you really think she'll come back a second time when we've withheld information?" Her voice was sharp, and Don shrank back from her sudden outburst. Perhaps she wasn't the vapid twink I'd originally pegged her for.

Maria held the papers out to me again. I reached for them, felt the static charge race up my arm at the first touch of skin to paper. These were more than simple paper; they held the weight of a child's burgeoning abilities.

The drawing on top was simple and reflected the pictures of India in my pocket: a stick girl with dark red hair and a circle drawn beside her head, a child's rendition of the orb in the pictures. The girl in the drawing was smiling. That was a good sign. As I flipped through the remainder of the stack, I quickly realized India wasn't only in trouble because she was missing; her powers were coming into their own earlier than they should have been, and they were beginning to drown her out. Each subsequent picture had an additional circle, and by the last picture, the little stick girl was covered by them, her face no longer smiling.

"She started drawing these the moment she could hold a crayon. Circles, always circles." Maria wrung her hands, and then fluttered them toward me. "We didn't know what to do. Do you really think you can find her?"

I held her gaze, knowing if she saw me look away at that moment, she would never completely believe me, she wouldn't trust me to find India. Without that trust, I would have the cops on my ass the whole way through this case and that was the last thing I needed. They'd just get in the way. Again.

"Yes, I can find her. There hasn't been a case yet where I haven't." *Liar liar pants on fire, Rylee*, my inner voice mocked me, hard.

Handing the drawings back to Maria, I asked, "Is there anything else I need to know?"

Maria shook her head and clutched the pictures to her chest.

"She likes tigers. Cats, all kinds of cats." Don came up behind his wife and placed his hands on her shoulders. "And she loves to braid things, hair, thread, yarn. Even paper."

I let him talk; let him think he was helping. Maria caught my eye and I shook my head—no need to cut him off at the knees. She gave the briefest of nods, and for a moment I felt a mild connection with the woman, but I immediately pushed it away. I didn't like getting attached to the parents. I was here for the kid, not them. Besides, the lack of attachment made it easier to be the bearer of bad news, which did happen more often than I liked.

"You have the account number to deposit the down payment?" I already knew the answer.

Maria nodded. "Half now, half when you bring her home."

Yup, that was me, taking money to find people's kids; but at least I did that, I was no charlatan taking money for hope and never delivering.

I left them holding onto each other, watching me—their only hope to regain their daughter—walk down the carpeted hallway and step into the stairwell. I didn't wave, and neither did they.

2

Besides the cool, constantly blowing wind that was North Dakota waiting for me to step outside, there were also two FBI agents. My usual stalker, O'Shea, and what appeared to be another new partner. Imagine that. Considering O'Shea's lack of people skills, it was no surprise. He went through partners like a woman changes her clothes.

"Adamson." O'Shea barked at me.

I flinched at the use of my surname, a name I didn't use anymore. Not since I'd started searching for kids nearly ten years ago.

His partner, a shorter version of O'Shea, I barely noticed. No angry vibes coming off that one. With O'Shea as his partner, I suspected he was taking a regular dose of Ativan just to get through the day. I would be, if I were in his shoes.

"What?" My distant teenage persona came to the surface with the snap back. He *really* brought out the best in me. He didn't look like your typical Irishman, with his dark eyes and hair. But his temper fit. Standing at least 6'3", he was one of very few men able to intimidate me. And it wasn't just his height, or the size of his muscled body, it was the history between us. For ten years he'd been trying to pin murder charges on me, and for ten years I'd stayed free. It rubbed him the wrong way for some reason.

Milly, my closest friend and confidant, long ago suggested I try flirting with him, to freak him out and throw him off his game. Lately I'd been considering it. I'd tried just about everything else and I really just wanted him off my case. Milly insisted it would work, and since she was the sex goddess in our duo, I could probably take her word for it. Problem was I wasn't sure I could pull it off.

"I know what you're doing. Stay the hell out of FBI business or I'll have you up on charges so fast even your ditzy little head will spin," O'Shea said, using his height to loom over me, like a bully on a playground trying to intimidate the little kids. Wrong chick to pull that move on; you'd think he would have learned that by now.

"Tell me something," I said, acting totally unimpressed, hiding my nerves. "If this is just a regular case, just a kid gone missing, why is the illustrious FBI on it?" I strolled to my Jeep, the two men following a few feet behind me. "Could it be that unlike most people whose children go missing, this family has money and can buy the really good help?" I looked over my shoulder to see their reactions to my words.

Both agents flushed at the implication. Mini-Me stepped into the ring next, ready for his shot at me. "The FBI can't be bought, Ms. Adamson."

"Really?" I smiled at him sweetly, turning to face the men, my hand on the Jeep's handle. "That's not what I heard. In fact, I heard when you've got lots of money or fame, that's when the FBI steps in." I paused, took my hand off the door and shook my head. "Glory hounds seeking the spoils of others' sorrow." So much for flirting.

O'Shea stepped close and held my door closed, once more looming over me. I didn't often feel small, but this close to him I felt like a child. The same child he'd met nearly ten years ago. "Adamson, one of these days I'm going to find out how you did it, how you made your little sister disappear. And when I do, all this vigilante shit of yours will stop because I'll make sure you're in jail for a very, *very* long time. You're not fooling me. I know who's to blame for your sister's death. We may not have a body, but one day soon, you're going to slip up."

My jaw tightened and tears threatened to show themselves. I would *not* let him see me cry, damn it. After all these years, he was the only one who could bring me this close to tears. "And when I do, you'll be there, right? You'll be there to slip the noose over my neck and watch me swing?"

He growled an obscenity and suddenly, we were nose to nose; Mini-Me was in the background muttering about people starting to stare.

"You'd think the FBI would like a little help finding kids and returning them to their families," I said, holding my ground.

"Not when they're dead!" He hissed at me, his hot minty breath flooding my nose. That had been the last kid. I'd found him, but it had been too late. The family was grateful to have closure. The FBI and local police, not so much. It's a little difficult to explain a werewolf attack to people who have no idea the monsters are real. Of course, there had been other kids that hadn't made it home alive, but I didn't tell O'Shea. No need to point out that detail.

"At least I can find them! More than you slackers ever manage," I snarled back. I hoped my breath smelled bad. Damn, would flirting with this man really work?

"Slackers?" His voice got soft, and I knew I touched a raw spot. I couldn't help poking some more at it.

"Glorified donut-eating cops. The only difference is you get to dress in Gucci, and the cops have hand-me-down uniforms."

His eyes nearly bugged out, and he grabbed me by the shoulders. I went limp in his hands. "Assault on an unarmed woman, O'Shea? Now that won't look good on the old permanent record, will it?"

He didn't drop his hands, not right away. "Since when do you go anywhere without your blades?" He took his hands off my shoulders and flipped my jacket open; his fingers brushed underneath my breasts even, sending a shot of awareness through me, the perv. I let him. I certainly wasn't going to tell him all my weapons were waiting for me in the Jeep. But I had nothing on me at the moment.

Wiping his hands on his pants, as if he'd touched something nasty, he said, "I know what you are, Adamson. You're a fraud and a child killer."

I'd had enough of his tirade, enough of the memories he stirred up. I leaned forward until we were nose to nose again, and gave him the eye contact I knew most people couldn't handle. It was time to put

Milly's suggestion to the test. When you have chocolate eyes laced with gold and emerald green, it either freaks people out or turns them on. I was banking on them freaking him out.

"You know what I think, Agent O'Shea?" He blinked at me and I took advantage of the proximity of his lips. I planted a big fat kiss on him, slipping my tongue through his teeth and flicking it along the roof of his mouth. He didn't fight me, and for a split second his lips softened on mine, the taste of mint lingering on my tongue as I pulled away from him. O'Shea swayed, and then scrambled away from me, dark eyes wide. His hand went to his gun.

"I think you just like to follow me around so you can watch my nice tight ass wiggle. You've been watching it for nearly ten years, haven't you?" I blew a kiss at Mini-Me and hopped into my Jeep.

The kiss did what nothing else could have, what nothing in ten years had managed. It shut him up. Well shit, Milly was right. I left from our encounter whistling a tune, a smile on my lips.

"Slackers," O'Shea shouted, and then muttered under his breath when Martins, his new partner, scuttled away to his desk with wide eyes. O'Shea knew he was the talk of the office, knew the other Agents looked sideways at him for taking this obsession with Adamson to a whole new level. Ten years he'd followed her, ten years he'd learned her habits, her training, even her taste in food. All so he could drag her down. He didn't care what the other agents thought, never had, but knew it made life just that much more difficult when it came to getting the higher ups to agree to requisitions. Taking slow breaths, O'Shea calmed himself, not wanting to admit the true reason for his anger.

That kiss had set him on fire. He could still feel it, the pressure of her lips, the dainty flick of her tongue over his. He let out a groan and slid into his chair. The worst thing possible for any officer of the law was to get hung up on a suspect, and that's what Adamson was, a suspect. It didn't matter that the case was cold. It didn't matter that there was literally no proof she'd killed her sister; he had a gut feeling something was off about her, and he was sticking with his instincts.

"Hey, partner."

O'Shea lifted his eyes to see Martins fiddling with his tie, nerves coming through with every twitch of his fingers. "I was thinking, maybe we should tail her. See where she goes."

Shaking his head, O'Shea pointed to a tracking device on his desk that blinked a muted red. "I've already tagged her Jeep. Goes on the fritz now and again, but we can follow her anywhere. If it's working."

Martins lit up like a freaking Christmas tree. "Awesome, let's go then."

God, O'Shea hated the young ones. Had he ever been that ridiculously eager? Like a dog just waiting to be set on a bird?

The last thing O'Shea wanted was to see Adamson again. Auburn hair, gold, green, and chocolate eyes that could skewer a man at ten paces, not to mention a body lean and hard from the rigorous regime she followed. He could still feel the brush of his hand under her breast, and he clenched his fingers to fight off the sensation.

Fuck! His pulse hammered. He'd been after her since she was sixteen; what had happened this time that was so different? He'd frisked her before. Running his hands through his hair, he tried to think about how she'd killed her little sister, but all he could see was the pain in her stunning eyes when he'd accused her of the crime. How soft and vulnerable she'd looked in that moment.

Adamson's little sister's body had never been recovered, but Adamson had run from the scene, gone into hiding for two weeks before they found her. Of course, they couldn't make any of the charges stick, but he'd been trained to see guilt. And that was the whole crux of it. Adamson was guilty. He knew it, she knew it; the only problem was he just couldn't prove it.

Making a decision, he stood up. "Martins, let's go. She's not going to slip past us this time."

No matter how good a kisser she was.

3

Before I went any further with the search, I did what had become more than a habit for me—something closer to a ritual. I had two stops to make. The first one was the local toy store, "Hannigans Shenanigans," where I purchased a large stuffed elephant. It was my required gift for the second location I was headed to.

The house I parked in front of could barely be called a house. A shanty or a shack was a better description; it had just enough insulation to make it through the coldest part of our winters here in the badlands. The whole thing was on a slant, tilted crazily to the left, seemingly propped up by the pile of junk reaching the eaves on that side of the house. The floorboards groaned under my weight and the smell of rotting wood filled my nose.

"That you, baby girl? I thought I told you not to come around till your momma cleaned you up some. Crazy blue socks everywhere." Her soprano voice echoed through the thin wood and I shook my head. Obviously not one of her more lucid days.

As far as adults went, Giselle was one of the few who had my sympathies. She was born with the ability to see a person's past, present, and probable future. But just like a carpenter that only has so many hammer swings in him before his elbow blows, she only had so many viewings in her before her mind broke.

There isn't a lot for me to say about Giselle. She's a broken woman, still in her prime, but aged prematurely by her calling in life. Since her mind wandered, there were very few people she would see, but she had an affinity for stuffed animals. And I didn't get all freaked out by the voices that showed up on occasion around her. Not ghosts, but some sort of leftover from the guides she'd acquired in life. Above all that, she was my mentor and the closest thing I had to a mother now.

"It's just me, Giselle. Rylee. I brought you a new stuffed toy. An elephant, I know you don't have one of those."

I pulled the large grey velvet-covered elephant from behind my back. She came to the screen door, and I got a good look at her. I hadn't seen her for some time; I'd been so busy with tracking that at least a month had gone by since our last visit, and the time hadn't been kind to her. She'd lost weight and there were patches of skin showing through her clothes, skin that was no longer a healthy pink, but mottled and age-spotted. Dirty blonde hair pulled back into a severe bun, stretching her features even more, leaving her sunken cheeks and vacant brown eyes the only thing noticeable. My heart sank at the sight of her. I didn't want to believe I was losing her to the madness, even though she'd warned me about it when she'd first taken me under her wing.

"Rylee? Ah, I remember now. Rylee. Yes, come inside dear; show me what you've brought for Giselle."

She shuffled away and I followed her in, breathing shallowly; trying not to think of all the possibilities for the smells. This was not good. Milly and I were going to have to do something about this, no matter how hard it might be. Giselle had raised the two of us; now we'd have to take care of her. Scattered junk littered the floor, old newspaper, bags of groceries un-emptied and stacks of books to the ceiling—and those were just the things I could identify. It was worse every time I came.

The back kitchen was as full as the rest of the house, only I suspected this was where the majority of the bad smells came from.

Giselle dusted off a rickety gold chair, circa 1960, and I sat down. She pulled a green vinyl chair with rips in it close and grabbed my hand before I could even ask her, her eyes suddenly focusing, as an intelligence that hadn't been there a moment before filled them.

Because I'm an Immune, even psychics can't read me; it's like I don't exist. But I have lines in my hand and reading those lines isn't really magic. It's more like knowing how to read a map and understand all the symbols and variances.

"Ah, little Rylee, you have big trouble coming your way. Always the same with you though." She turned my hand first one way, then the other, her grip intense.

"You will find someone, a man from your past, who will become a part of your future."

"You mean like a lover?" I hated the almost hopeful tone in my voice, the way it sounded, but I needed to be as clear as possible. A little romance never hurt anyone, but if it got in the way of finding India, or any other child for that matter, it wouldn't matter how I felt about him. In the back of my mind, I wondered if it was O'Shea and quickly pushed the thought away. One kiss did not a lover make him.

"Obsession." She whispered the word and a cool wind wrapped around my ankles. "Death. Power. They are all tangled here." She pointed to the middle of my hand where indeed, there seemed to be several lines tangled about one another. "But you will also find your own past in this circle of three."

The house groaned as a gust of wind pummeled the barely standing structure. I shivered and Giselle did too.

"You must go now. I have said enough for today. Where are your blue socks, child?" Her eyes slid into vacancy once more, and I grabbed her hands, snagging her attention.

I asked her what I always asked. "The child I seek, will I find her in time?"

Giselle's eyes flickered and the intelligence returned, though I could see it waver. "This child you seek, she is strong; you have time, I do not know if it will be enough, but you have time."

I stood to leave, pressing the stuffed elephant into her now-empty hands. For all that she loved her stuffed animals, I never once saw one after I had left it with her, and I still had no idea what she did with them. I brought them now because it was one of the few times I got to see her smile.

"Wait."

I froze in the hallway, Giselle's voice drawing me back in.

"There is another child, a child of golden sunshine and blue skies that seeks for you."

Every muscle in me tensed, my body paralyzed by the seer's words. It couldn't be what I thought, but I whispered her name without meaning to.

"Berget."

The cold wind whipped through the house again, papers scattering about, a stack of books toppling over, and chaos ensued.

Giselle scrambled to her feet and rushed past me, caterwauling like a banshee about blue socks, her hair coming loose from her bun and the strands of it whipping about her face, obscuring her features. She attempted to right the things the wind demolished. It only made matters worse; for every pile she straightened, another fell, taking two more with it.

I shook myself free of the paralysis and reached out for Giselle, grabbing her by her bony shoulders, shocked at how thin she'd become.

"Let me go, devil spawn! Blood seeker! Killer! Whore! Let me go!" I didn't take the names personally. Though some were accurate. You can't get too pissy when people are telling you the truth.

I hung onto her shoulders, steered her back into the kitchen and plunked her into the green chair. She went limp and a voice came softly to my ear. "Sing for her, child." I didn't look around; I knew it was one of her guides. They loved Giselle, and so I did what they said. I sang.

"*Trip upon trenchers, and dance upon dishes, my mother sent me for some barm, some barm; she bid me go lightly, and come again quickly, for fear the young men should do me some harm. Yet didn't you see, yet didn't you see, what naughty tricks they played on me? They broke my pitcher, spilt the water, cursed my mother, chided her daughter, and kissed my sister instead of me.*"

I trailed off, the old song from my childhood catching in my throat. They didn't call it a melancholy tune for nothing.

"So nice, dear. Perhaps you'll sing to me again sometime?" Giselle's coherent question surprised me, but I took it in stride.

"Of course, Giselle. Will you be all right now?"

She cocked her head and squinted her eyes at me. "Child, go home and get your blue socks; you'll need them before the week is out."

I left her there in her kitchen muttering about blue socks, the elephant gripped in her frail hands and a cool wind blowing through her house.

4

The older-style cell phone shook a little in my hand. I'd found if I held it just right it didn't crap out on me too often. Pinching the phone between thumb and forefinger, I squeezed until the power bar came on. Milly's number was normally embedded in my brain, but this time I had to look it up.

Millicent, Milly to her friends, was my closest friend and the other girl Giselle raised. The term *raised* gives the impression that we were little when she took us on. I was sixteen and Milly was a year younger. Both orphaned in our own ways, me twice, if you want to get picky, both of us needing a mentor for the innate abilities that were becoming apparent.

"Hello?" Her soft voice was raspy and it was obvious I'd pulled her from sleep.

"Hey, witch. Get out of bed. We've got a bit of a problem." I switched ears with the phone and turned the heat up with my now free hand. I could still feel the wind from Giselle's house in my bones.

She groaned. "Listen, I've barely been in bed for two hours. You know I don't run on the same schedule as most people."

I nodded and said, "I know, I wouldn't call if it wasn't important. It's Giselle. We need to get her out of that house. I have some money from this next case, but it won't be enough for a care home."

She gave a sharp gasp, and I heard the bed creak in the background, then a soft exclamation that wasn't Milly. I smiled. She was always having "sleepovers." That was something I didn't have the time for, or the inclination—at least right now. Matters of the heart were just too messy, in my opinion. I thought again about what Giselle said, about a man coming into my life. No, this was not the time for that kind of crap.

Footsteps and a door closing told me we had a little more privacy. "What's wrong?"

"We have to move her. I don't know how, but that house is falling down around her ears. And the madness has moved quickly in the last few months. I don't think she'll survive the winter on her own. She's lost a lot of weight." I paused and scanned the streets. "Hang on a minute, I think I'm lost."

I took a left turn and navigated through a sub-division. Bismarck wasn't a huge town, but it was expanding, and when all the houses were cookie cutter look a-likes, it was easy to get turned around.

Slowing for a stop sign, I continued. "I'm on a salvage right now." That was my word for going after kids, just in case we had anyone listening in. "I don't know how long it will be, at least a week maybe. If you can start to get Giselle out, I'll help you when I get back."

Silence on the other end of the line. "Milly? Are you still there?"

"Rylee, meet me at the coffee shop, the one on East Ave. I've got . . . news."

My phone took that moment to blink off, and no matter how I smashed and squeezed it I couldn't get it to flick back on.

"Damn!" I spun the wheel and did a tight u-turn. The coffee shop, "Bean Done Right," was about five minutes away. Another detour, but for Milly I would take it.

The parking lot was empty; in between breakfast and lunch the coffee shop slowed right down. Milly stood outside, arms wrapped around her upper body, dark brown hair pulled into a high ponytail. I waved and hopped out of the Jeep.

"Hey. What's going on?" I didn't ask her how she was; it was obvious. Upset, scared, uncertain. Which for Milly was odd. She was the one who was organized, always knew how to lay out a difficult salvage; rarely did her emotions get the better of her. Except the horny ones, that is.

"I can't help her, Rylee." Her green eyes flicked away from mine. "I can't be here for long, but I had to tell you in person."

Shock filtered through me. This wasn't like Milly, not at all. What the hell was going on? I didn't get a chance to ask before she rushed on and answered my unspoken question.

"The Coven wants me to break ties with all people who aren't witches. That includes you and Giselle. This is what I've always wanted. I'm so sorry."

Her eyes were swollen, her lips trembled, and her slight frame shook. I reached out to put a hand on her shoulder and she flinched as though I'd hit her.

"Do you mean like forever?" My voice came through on a whisper, my heart breaking at the thought of losing one more person in my life.

Her hiccupping sobs were all the answer I needed. I looked away from her, stared into the coffee shop, with the empty seats and the cashier staring out at me.

"What about the salvages? Can you walk away from them?" What I was really asking, what we both knew I meant was, could she walk away from kids who'd been like us: alone, searching for a home, for a safe haven, broken souls who would need mending.

She covered her face with her hands. "I can't have"— she hiccupped another sob— "both. I can't have the Coven and . . . you and Giselle. This is hard for me. They offered me this spot a month ago."

That would explain her absence lately.

I would beg if I had to. On this case, more than any other, I needed her and I would fight to keep her as my friend. "This girl was taken from Deerborn Park. Just like Berget, even the same day as her. Milly, please." I stepped closer to her. Again she flinched. "Please help me this one last time."

Tears tracked down her face and her eyes lifted to meet mine, only to drop again. Shoulders slumped, and she continued to cry. "I'm . . . sorry. I know how hard it is for you to face this . . . now. But–" She twitched as I stepped closer.

That was enough of that. If she was going to be afraid of me, then I'd give her a reason. I grabbed her arms and shook her. "You took an oath, the same as I did, to find these missing kids. You promised, you selfish bitch!" I bit the words, anger making me mean.

"You're hurting me," she said, but didn't try to pull away.

"Good, that makes two of us." Still, I dropped my hands and backed up, shaking my head. A slow deep breath calmed my racing heart. "They shouldn't try to take you away, that isn't right."

"It's how they do things," she said, rubbing her arms. "I've got to go. They can't know that I've seen you."

Milly turned her back and walked away from me, pausing at the edge of the building. "Goodbye, Rylee." The tears in her voice did me in.

"You can always come home, Milly. No matter what, you know that right? I'll always look out for you." It was the best I could do. My own emotions were choking me. I didn't want to be left behind again.

Her words hitched into sobs. I couldn't be truly angry with her. We both had wanted only one thing growing up: to fit in. And now she had a chance, and I couldn't begrudge her that, no matter how much it hurt. Swallowing the pain back, I slipped into the Jeep. "You'll always be my witch, Milly." I pulled the door closed, shutting out the wind and my best friend. Only then did I let the tears fall and allow myself to feel the pain of being abandoned once again.

5

I didn't have time to relocate my mentor if I was to save India. But there was no way I was going to let Giselle stay in her house with what felt like an early winter coming on, and I didn't have the funds to put her up in a care home; they were too expensive and the wait to get in was long. Maybe after this job I would move her out to my place; but then I immediately dismissed the thought. Giselle didn't like to leave her home, never had, even when her mind had been mostly intact. This was about to get difficult.

I wove back through the subdivision to Giselle's house and parked out front for the second time that day.

Bundling her up in a threadbare lightweight jacket, I tucked her into the passenger seat of the Jeep and cranked the heat up.

Her eyes followed me, a silent question in them, as I walked around to my side of the vehicle.

"We're going for a ride," I said, as I put on my seatbelt and pulled away from the curb. She huddled in her seat, lost in her mind's abyss, somewhere far beyond my reach.

She'd been the one to name me, name my abilities. I was an Immune and a Tracker all bundled up into one. My tracking abilities hadn't come on line until after Berget went missing. Since then, I could pinpoint anyone I was close with, friends and even strangers, when I worked at it. All I needed was their name and a picture of them, and I was off and running. Could lead you right to them, no matter the distance. More than that, I knew if they were hurt, happy, sad, alive, or dead. With the kids I hunted for, this ability was priceless. It only failed me if the kids weren't on this side of the Veil, which from time to time was the case. If they'd been taken by supernaturals interested in the kid's powers and abilities, they weren't kept where I could find them easily. Even if they were dead, I could still track them, to at least give the parents some sense of closure. Unfortunately, that was all too often the case. The only one I'd never been able to find was Berget. I reached for her, even as I thought of this anomaly, finding only an empty spot inside my skull where she should have been. Even if she was dead, I should have been able to find her, to bring her home.

My thoughts flickered as I glanced over at Giselle, sound asleep and snoring lightly, a blush of color on her cheeks. I reached over and brushed my hand over her forehead, letting out a sigh of relief. "No fever."

I took a left turn and my mind went back to the day I'd been bitten by a large rattlesnake, not long after moving in with Giselle and Milly. We'd been in the backyard, me practicing my tracking on the neighborhood children, pinpointing them for Giselle, while Milly practiced her incantations under her breath. I'd stepped back into a large bush and felt a sharp jab into my left leg. Looking down, a massive diamond shaped head hung off my left calf, venom pumping into my system. Its eyes transfixed me as it worked its teeth deeper into my flesh, trying to get a better grip on my calf.

Giselle shouted, but I was too frozen by shock to move. A large part of me thought it was my time to die; the guilt over losing Berget still sat heavily on me, my inability to track the one child I loved more than any other, the depression it invoked was something I couldn't escape. However, it wasn't yet my time to die.

That was the day Giselle told me I was an Immune, something she'd been suspecting, but hadn't known for sure until I'd been bit. I was Immune not just to the supernatural bites that could turn me furry or sunlight hating, but immune to poisons of all kinds. I was also immune to most, but not all, magic and was invisible to most psychic probing. It was a sweet deal and not a part of my nature many people knew about. It was an ace up my sleeve when hunting for kids. The supernaturals who'd taken them didn't know I wouldn't be affected by their spells, bites, and incantations. Yay for genetic throwbacks.

We pulled up to the hospital and I parked on the curb, getting Giselle as close to the door as possible.

"Here we are." I opened the passenger door.

At first, she looked surprised to see me. Then she smiled and said, "Did you find your blue socks, dear?"

I shook my head. "I was hoping you could help me find them. I think I left them here." I pointed to the hospital.

She squinted in the direction of my hand. "You think you left them in a hospital?"

I blushed. This would not be a good time for her to be more lucid. When she was angry, she could give O'Shea a run for his money.

"Yes, the hospital. I think that's where they are. Can you help me?" I hoped to just get her inside.

Giselle followed me in through the sliding front doors and up to the reception desk without a word, lowering herself slowly into one of the padded chairs set out for the infirm. I watched her a moment before turning to the clerk. "I'd like to admit my friend. She's not competent and I think she may be quite sick. Maybe an infection of some sort. She's been hanging around the neighbors who just got back from Mexico." That got the clerk's attention real fast, what with all the upheaval of the swine flu coming up from down south. Of course, it wasn't true, but I didn't want them pissing around with whether or not to admit her and for how long. Just the possibility of swine flu was an automatic admittance for someone Giselle's age, and a minimum of a one-week observation around here.

Within moments, they had Giselle under quarantine, settled into a private room, on fluids and a heavy dose of sedatives to keep her quiet.

I stood by her side, mask over my nose and mouth, holding her bare hands with my gloved ones. "I'll be back as quick as I can," I whispered, knowing she couldn't hear me anyway. The week of warmth and good food would help her more than anything else, and having her in the hospital would keep me from worrying when I should be focusing on India.

Leaning in, I gave her a kiss on the cheek through the paper mask, then started out the door.

"Milly will come back, Rylee."

I spun back toward her. "What?" But her eyes were closed and her breathing was even, her body slumped with sleep. There was nothing more, and again I headed out the door. Maybe I was hearing things, or maybe I was just hearing things I wanted to hear.

6

Again, I worked my way through the subdivision, this time with a distinctive shadow behind me. A traditional FBI dark-cultured SUV trailing at a distance of no more than three car lengths followed me through all the twists and turns. For now, I ignored them, but at some point I was going to have to do something about them. Damn O'Shea, he was going to make things difficult right off the bat this time.

I pulled up to a small green-trimmed house, a two-story, with a perfectly manicured lawn out front. The only concession to living in a more rural part of the country was the Christmas lights that were still up from last year.

Leaving my Jeep, I made my way around the side of the house and through the perfect, non-rusty gate in the perfectly trimmed white fence. The basement was a separate suite and was rented out to Kyle Jacobs, an eighteen-year old computer geek fresh out of high school who also happened to be the best hacker in town. Make that the best hacker, period.

Not bothering to knock, I let myself right in. If Kyle didn't know you or didn't like you, the door would be locked. He had the whole place bugged with cameras and recorders and the door could be locked with a simple remote control he kept with him at his work desk. The kid was more paranoid than an alcoholic who'd "seen" someone looking at them sideways.

The hallway was bare of any personal things; a camera was up in the far corner tracking my movements. I waved at it and Kyle called to me from his workroom.

"Come on in, Rylee." I followed his voice through the kitchen full of unwashed plates, open chip bags and empty root beer cans into the workroom, what had once been a living room. Computers, at least four that I could see, two laptops, multiple cameras, a crazy amount of wires, and other pieces of electronics I couldn't identify were set up throughout. I touched nothing, hung back from the equipment. The thing was, the closer I got, the more the technology would act up and I needed it to work.

I made my way to the "client's" chair and eased myself into it. It had started life as a La-Z-Boy recliner. Now, the handle was broken and the seat tried to suck you in and eat you if you sat down too hard. I'd found that out the first time I'd come for a visit.

"You want a beer?" He held out a can of root beer to me. His blond hair hung just past his pale blue eyes encased in big glasses. He was a cute kid, but looked closer to thirteen than the eighteen he was.

I shrugged, "Sure, pass one over." I cracked it open, took a sip, and damn near choked. "No wonder you have so much energy, kid." The sugar rush was immediate, lighting up my adrenaline. I was more than a tad bit sensitive to the stuff, but once in a while I liked to indulge. I put the can on the floor at my feet. There was no way I'd be able to finish it.

Kyle laughed and clicked a button on his mouse. The screen lit up. "The usual, going through police files?"

"Yeah, but I have a tail today so they may be trying to trace your work."

He spun back to me. "What kind of tail?"

"FBI."

His eyes widened, and he half choked on a mouthful of pop. "What?" He squeaked out.

I nodded, confirming what I'd already said.

"And you came here? Man, I could get so busted for the hacking I do!" He was close to shouting, his eyes even wider behind the glasses.

I shushed him with a wave of my hand. "Have you ever been caught?" I already knew the answer.

"No, but it's because I'm careful." Frowning, he stared down at the keyboard. "This could mean jail time, easy. I don't think I can do this. Not today."

From past experience, I knew getting angry was a last resort with him. He could be intimidated, but that would make it harder to work with him later on. "Listen, the little girl I'm looking for, she was stolen from the same park as another child." I paused, debating how much to tell him. Licking my lips, I held my breath, then slowly let it out. "She's gone missing from the same park as my little sister, same date, same situation. I need this info, Kyle. Please." I lifted my eyes to his, hoping he could see how important this was. "I have to find her, I can't lose her after not being able to find . . ." I swallowed hard, the sudden lump in my throat making it difficult to breathe. Reaching for the can of root beer, I took a swig, wishing it was alcohol and not pop.

His chair squeaked. "So that's why you do this, huh? I've always wondered."

"My past is not a required discussion for my contacts. You told me cash was all I had to give you." Putting the can of pop back down at my feet, I spread my hands in front of me. "Are you going to help me?"

Fingers flew across the keyboard. He pulled up surveillance cameras even I didn't know he had of the whole street and the next one over. Sure enough, at the end of his street sat the SUV, two dark suits inside. I felt like waving to them, knowing it was more than likely O'Shea was one of said dark suits.

Kyle turned back to me. "I thought maybe you were joking. Okay, I guess I was hoping you were messing with me." His eyes suddenly looked far older than they had just a moment before.

I shook my head. "No, I wasn't. What will it be? Helping me find this kid, or sending me out on my own?"

He snorted and ran a hand through his straw-colored hair. "Okay, I can get you in, but as always, we don't know each other if you get picked up."

I smiled, relief coursing through me. I put two fingers in the air. "Scouts' honor."

I gave him India's information and within a few minutes he had it pulled up. There in black 'and white and color was what I was worried about.

There was always a small chance something got left behind by the kidnappers, even supernaturals fucked up from time to time. But in this case, there was literally no evidence there had even been a kidnapping other than the fact there was a child missing. No footprints, cloth samples, or eye witnesses to be found, despite the fact she went missing at sunset, just before dark, under her own mother's care at a busy park. It was exactly like Berget.

Like being transported back in time, I could see my sister on the swing, laughing and squealing, the fading sun turning her hair into a golden nimbus around her head. I was lying on my back, reading my book, glancing up from time to time. Between one pump of her little legs and the next, she was snatched. I closed my eyes against the guilt and pain swelling through me. I wouldn't let India face the same fate as Berget.

Pushing the memories aside, I thought about the case I was working now. I was definitely going to need some outside help on this one. With Milly out, the closest shaman with any actual ability was in New Mexico. A bit of a drive, but I really had no other choice in the matter.

"You think you can find this kid, even though it's the same as your sister's case?"

Kyle's question caught me off guard. "Yes, I can find her." I had to believe it. Giselle told me there was time. Scanning the screen, I read through her case. Not a single hint as to what had taken her. Nothing. Yet, if it was truly the same as Berget, I had an idea of what it might be, though not who. Why would the FBI be brought in? Just because there was money involved? Was there a slew of kidnappings going on? A chill ran down my spine. Or maybe there was another reason entirely; maybe they were starting to wonder about the crimes that couldn't be solved, the ones that were impossible unless supernatural reasons were taken into account. Not that they thought like that.

I pulled out a wad of hundred dollar bills and laid five on the table, Kyle's usual fee. I laid another ten on top, almost half of my deposit from India's parents. "Can you get me into the FBI's files?"

Kyle stared at the money, and looked up at me. "Maybe, yeah, I could. But what do they have to do with this? I can't go hacking the FBI just because you want me to."

I leaned forward, my hands going to either side of him and effectively pinning him up against his desk. Kyle's eyes widened and not in a good way.

"I always have a good reason, kid. That doesn't mean I can always tell you. You don't get to know everything just because you're my hacker." I was always good at the bitch eyes—you know, the drop-dead and leave me alone eyes that every girl acquires at some point or another—and today was no exception. The air crackled between us and I shifted my body so he got a glimpse of one of the blades on my hip.

He nodded and turned around, completely silent. I felt like an absolute bully, but that didn't mean I'd apologize. I would make up for it another time. Maybe bring him a new video game.

It took Kyle close to ten minutes and some serious typing to get into the FBI files, but he cracked the codes. "You're only going to have a few minutes to find what you're looking for before I get traced." His voice was all business now.

He gave me his seat. And I started searching, hoping my proximity to the computer wouldn't crash it. Today was my lucky day. There was a file under India's name, and one under Berget's. A large file under my own that I scanned quickly, but there was no mention of supernatural abilities.

"You've got two minutes left," Kyle said from behind me.

"Okay, I'm almost there," I said

I did a search for 'supernatural,' and then 'unexplained,' with no results. "What's another word for unexplainable or magic?" I muttered to myself.

"Arcane." Kyle grumbled at me. He was still pouting from being told to butt out.

I typed in the word and the computer screen flashed before taking me to a section I hoped I would never see. The Arcane Division of the FBI.

7

"You have got to be freaking kidding me!" Kyle exclaimed over my shoulder.

"Damn it, kid, don't you ever listen?" I snapped. "Forget it, just print this off, or save it for me, or do whatever you can in the last bit of time you have."

Kyle sat and the printer started up. "I've printed the entire section for you, but it's over three hundred pages long so it's going to take a while."

"How long's 'a while,' and are you going to have enough paper?" I sat back in the recliner.

A while turned out to be over two hours thanks to his prehistoric printer. You'd think with all the up-graded equipment he had, he would've put out for a faster printer. The possibility of not having enough paper was bad, but worse was his non-stop questions, of which I answered zero. If he'd been just a few years older, I would have had a lot less difficulty with him. I would have just thumped him on the head and left him tied up in the bathroom. Being a kid gave him an immunity to my anger and my blades that he didn't even realize he had.

I ended up drinking the rest of the root beer and felt a sugar headache coming on fast. At least it would keep me awake.

Kyle bundled up all the papers for me and wrapped them with two elastic bands. "Here, I think that's all of them."

I took the bundle and tucked it under one arm.

"So, what do you think the files are really for?"

I looked up, surprised at first. Of course, he couldn't believe the files were about the supernatural. That was an impossibility in his world of technology.

"Just a code name for missing kids. The ones they can't explain." He followed me out to the door, neither one of us noticing the slight beeping on his security system until we were at the door. Or the pair of suits walking up on the camera monitors toward his back door. Not good; sloppy on both our parts. I blamed my inattention to the memories that this case was stirring up.

The doorknob was cool under my hand and the slightest shuffle on the other side of the door caught my ear at the last second. I froze and looked over at Kyle.

His face was pale and his eyes wide. He shook his head ever so slightly and I backed off the door. Together, we sidled back into the kitchen. Running back to his workroom, he checked his security monitors and let out a groan, hands clenched in his hair. There in black and white were two very dark grey suits, standing at his back door, discussing something. Probably us. Kyle grabbed my arm, his body trembling. "I didn't know they would actually show up at my door," he whispered, his voice cracking under the sudden stress.

"Neither did I." I thought for a minute. There was a way out of this, but there was a possibility Kyle would get a glimpse at some of the things I could do. "Go back into your computer room, get all the online games going that you can, quick now." I gave him a shove in the direction of his work room.

"How's that going to help?"

"Just do what I say!" I took a breath and explained quickly. "If they come in, you can claim you didn't see what I was doing, that you were playing your games while I used the printer." A thread of adrenaline started to pump through me. If I got thrown in jail, it would mean the end of India's chances. I couldn't let that happen.

Kyle stumbled over his own feet as he tried to make his body obey his commands despite his obvious fear, glancing back at me for reassurance. I nodded and shooed at him with my free hand before turning my back on him.

With Kyle busy, I turned my attention to the bundle of papers. I couldn't make it disappear; that was way beyond what I could do. But I could make it look like something else. Something close to what it truly was. Giselle had shown me how to do this, but using my abilities to do something they weren't designed to do would make my sugar headache a fond memory.

Concentrating, I focused on the heading, slowing my breathing to match the pulse of my energy. FBI Arcane Division became Francine Bouvier's Interesting Facts on Divisions of the Arcane. A bead of sweat rolled down my face. This kind of glamour always left me drained. It just wasn't one of my strong abilities, though at the moment I was glad I at least had this little amount. I slipped off the elastic bands and flipped through the pages; changed the major headings of which there were ten. The pages began to flow under my hands as the glamour took hold and spread through the entire stack of paper. I let out a breath and wiped the sweat off my forehead with the back of my hand. Crap I was tired now, even with the sugar rush; I was not at my best for facing down an FBI agent. Even worse, since it was O'Shea.

A hard knock at the door snapped my head up. A glance at Kyle's white face and wide eyes didn't give me much comfort.

"Stay there," I said, gesturing at Kyle as he stood. "I'll go to the door and deal with them. You just stay there." He nodded and sank back into his chair, his hands going to the keyboard, listless with his fear. If O'Shea saw Kyle, he'd know there was more to this than what I was going to tell him. I took a deep breath and strode across to the door, Francine Bouvier's Interesting facts clutched in my arms. One last deep breath and I opened the door, smiling up into O'Shea's glowering face. "Well hello, Agent O'Shea, fancy meeting you here."

I leaned against the doorframe, paper bundle held loosely in my arms, as if it were not important at all. "If I didn't know better, I'd say you were following me." I looked up at him from under my eyelashes. "In fact, I'm beginning to think you want a repeat of this morning." I ran my tongue over my bottom lip.

His face cultured under his olive complexion. Oh yeah, he hadn't forgotten. If only I'd tried this trick of

Milly's years ago. He regained his composure quickly, though I did detect a smirk on his partner's face. No doubt Mini-Me had been razzing O'Shea relentlessly about kissing a person of interest.

"What are you doing here, Adamson?" O'Shea growled at me.

I blinked up at him. "Me? I'm visiting a friend. He has a printer." I shifted the bundle of papers to get his attention. "I don't have any high tech stuff like computers. Prefer to have things on hard copy. I don't think that's against the law now, is it?"

Mini-Me piped up. "Of course not, miss. We're just doing our duty, following up on leads." His voice trailed off as O'Shea turned his glare on his partner.

I continued to smile as O'Shea's glare returned to me, letting the laughter fill my eyes. His dark eyes narrowed. I started to chuckle. Couldn't help it. I fanned my face and took some deep, gulping, over-exaggerated breaths. "Oh man, you two are way too much fun! Do you hire out, or do you only do your act for friends and persons of interest?"

They were both frowning at me now, and O'Shea reached out and snagged the bundle of papers. I heard a squeak from inside the house and silently prayed for Kyle to hold it together for a few more minutes.

O'Shea glanced over the heading of the bundle of paper and flipped through a few pages. "You catching up on some light reading?"

I shrugged. "I'll read anything. Especially when I have nothing better to do." I gave him my best innocent eyes, keeping them wide and batting my lashes.

An exaggeration for sure, but we both knew I was lying; he just couldn't prove it.

He snorted and handed the papers back to me. We also both knew he didn't have a warrant for anything, so unless they traced the hacker here already, which I didn't think they had, there wasn't any reason for him to continue harassing me.

"Are we about done?" I asked.

"Not by a long shot, Adamson. Not by a very long shot." He turned on his heel and strode away, Mini-Me following in his wake.

Kyle shuffled up behind me. "You know those guys?"

"The big guy has been following me around for nearly ten years. You get kinda used to it."

"But they're FBI. Why would they follow you around?" Kyle's voice trailed off and I looked over my shoulder at him. He was just a kid—brilliant, dorky, and so naive it almost hurt to look at him. I told him the truth though; he deserved that much from me.

"They think I did a very bad thing, that I killed my sister. And some days, I think they're right. I could have stopped those who took her, if I'd been trained then."

I stepped into the bright sunlight, the cold cut of the wind going right through me.

8

I drove for an hour, heading west before I pulled off the interstate and into a gas station, just as the autumn sun began to set. I was too far from home to make it before I'd just have to get up and leave again in the morning. It was better to get a good night's sleep and start fresh in the morning—that's what Giselle always said.

There was a motel across the street, halfway decent, clean, and close to the highway. I'd stayed there before when I hadn't wanted to make the three-hour trek from Bismarck all the way home. All fuelled up, I pulled a U-turn and crossed the street, glad I always kept an overnight bag in my Jeep alongside an array of weapons and equipment not so easily found at a corner drug store. A girl can never be too prepared.

North Dakota is known for its farming, badlands, and good people. Not so much for its high-end hotels, gourmet cuisine, or anonymity. This little motel was no exception. Hiding my body from prying eyes, I slipped my favorite weapon into place: a two-foot long blade, edged in silver and copper, with a custom-fit handle just for me. No, I wasn't going hunting for vampires and I hadn't read too many comic books as a kid. But, most supernatural creatures weren't bothered by modern weaponry. It tended to piss them off rather than do any actual harm. Handle down near my right hip and blade tip near my left shoulder blade, it was held in place across my back, not only by sheaths and leather, but by a spell put together for me by Milly. My throat closed up as I thought of my sister-friend. That's what we'd been for nearly ten years; now she was just gone. I took a deep breath and let it out, putting her out of my mind as I examined the rest of my tools. Ten daggers, also edged in silver and copper, two lariats, one tazer, and one high-powered crossbow with bolts on top. Underneath, there were packages of herbs and poultices, again prepared by Milly, to use on everything from burns, cuts, and broken bones to head injuries. With everything accounted for and my blade underneath my jacket and securely in place, I went to check in.

The desk clerk nodded at me as I walked in, his battered cowboy hat pulled low over his ears and a few stray grey hairs sticking out at the edges. John had checked me in here more than once.

"Find any kids today, Ry?" He was also the only person I let get away with shortening my name; he was, after all, in his eighties and I figured he'd earned his right to say whatever he wanted to at his age.

"Nope, not today. Kissed an FBI agent, though. That was kind of fun." I winked at him and he smiled back at me. It was a routine game between us. I told him the truth and he thought I was funning him.

"Did you make him blush?"

I scooped my room key off the counter. "Come on, John, you know a lady's not supposed to kiss and tell.

Then again, I'm not much of a lady, so yes, I made him blush and his partner too. Too hot to handle—you should know that about me by now, John."

He guffawed and said, "Off with you now, girl. I swear, an FBI agent?"

I stepped back out into the quickly cooling night air and walked down to my unit. Number thirteen. I liked it, and it was the one everybody else avoided so I didn't have to worry about how many people had left their little nasty bits behind in the communal bed. Gross, I know, but something to think about next time you stay in a hotel.

It was still early, so I sat down at the small but real wooden desk, pulled out a pen and paper, and began to write down what I knew so far. At the top of the page I put India's name, age, hair, and eye color, suspected abilities, and quirks her parents told me about. I had nothing else to speculate on except what groups could possibly want her and her abilities as a spirit seeker. That had been my first inclination when I saw the pictures—someone who could commune with the dead with great ease and for whom the dead held a great affection. Like someone who was good with animals, spirit seekers rarely had to actually seek out spirits; the dead came to them, flocked to them in droves, desperate to be heard and remembered. There were times that it was a temporary phenomenon. Children had been known to grow out of their abilities as they hit puberty. But those who didn't were powerful and very, very rare.

I scrubbed my hands back through my hair and laid my head on the desk, on the paper with all of India's stats. "Where are you kid?" She didn't answer, not that I really expected her to. I hated the fact that I couldn't track a child on the other side of the Veil. My stomach growled suddenly, reminding me I hadn't eaten since breakfast. Leaving off with the list making, I headed out for something to stave off starvation.

There were no pizza joints out this way, or any other type of foods that could be delivered, so I settled for gas station gourmet. A bag of chips, two pepperoni sticks, and small carton of milk. Carbs, protein, and dairy, a nice balanced meal. The night air felt good, cleansing, with the constant wind that was just a part of the landscape, and I found myself walking away from the hotel, taking a side street into the nearest suburbs.

I walked for over an hour, my growling stomach and the food in my bag forgotten as my mind tried to work through what I was facing. If I wasn't on a salvage, I'd be doing everything I could to find out more about the Arcane Division of the FBI. How much did they know about the supernatural world, and was any of it true? But more than that, did they even have an inkling of how ugly it would get if the big, bad, uglies of the supernatural world felt threatened? It would be one giant clusterfuck if word got out about this new FBI division. It was a weight on me that only added to my concern over India. Distraction wasn't a possibility, not when going after a kid. So, for now I would have to put it aside, deal with it after I found her.

With the decision made on how I was going to handle at least that part of things, I headed back to the motel.

I poked my head back into the office before I went back to my room. "Hey, John. If anyone comes looking for me, dial me up first, would you?"

John frowned and scratched his head under his hat before answering. "Ain't nobody come looking for you before. You 'specting trouble?"

I shrugged and bit off a piece of pepperoni. "Maybe. Hopefully not, I've got a long day ahead of me tomorrow and don't really feel like spending the evening fighting off FBI agents, no matter how cute they are."

His laughter followed me back out the door and I could still hear him when I got to number thirteen—where the door stood open, the lock busted, splinters of wood scattered on the floor. Dropping my meager dinner and drawing my blade, I edged up to the door, keeping my back flat against the wall. For a good two minutes I was silent; I didn't move, just listened.

There was nothing, not a single heartbeat, breath, shuffle, or even any psychic energy thrumming through the air. I stepped into the room, still in a fighting stance, blade at the ready, despite what all my senses told me. I wished now I'd brought some of my other toys from the Jeep. I hadn't really been thinking anyone would be gunning for me. Not yet anyway. No one in the supernatural community should have known that I was on the case. By tomorrow, yes, but not by tonight. With only one large weapon between me and hand-to-hand fighting, I was not a happy girl, no matter how good my hand-to-hand was.

A quick circuit of the room showed nothing, confirming what I already knew: it was empty, the intruder gone. I let out a sigh. Nothing like a pile of problems to make life interesting.

Then something fluttered to my left. I turned to get a closer look. The curtain had been shredded and was covered in long black hair. I recognized it immediately. It belonged to a very large and very determined werewolf.

Damn it all to hell and back.

I lowered my blade and felt the itch in my spine a split second too late as a hairy set of claw-tipped hands wrapped themselves around my throat. I let out a strangled squawk, my hands first going for the claws, and then stopping to lower my blade.

I couldn't use it, not on this one.

9

"Gotcha!" A familiar rough voice growled in my ear as the hands tightened around my throat for a heartbeat before letting go. I took a deep breath and turned to see my ever faithful werewolf, half crouched at my feet, tongue lolling out; amber eyes wide and innocent, and his human wolf hybrid body covered in pitch black silver tipped hair.

I let out a sigh, a mixture of irritation and relief. It could have been worse; it could have been whatever had taken India on my tail, or even O'Shea and Mini-Me.

"Good job, you did it, you finally snuck up on me. But what are you doing all the way out here, so far away from home?" I lay my blade on the bed and folded my arms across my chest, doing my best imitation of a scolding mother and repeated my question. "Alex, what are you doing so far from home?"

He cringed, his body, stuck between human and wolf because he wasn't strong enough, and never would be, to switch between forms. Only the Alphas could do that; only the Alphas could pass for human. Most of the pack was like Alex, unable to switch between forms. To the contrary of what the world will tell you, being bit by a werewolf doesn't automatically make you a powerhouse. It only strengthens the traits you already have, takes them to the next level.

From what I could find out about his previous life, when Alex had been bitten he was a kind, quiet, submissive, harmless man. So he'd become the golden retriever version of a werewolf—loving and faithful.

He showed up on my doorstep one night, mauled half to death by his own pack members, and has been with me ever since. The pack didn't approve, and we were still dealing with the ramifications of that.

He sat on his haunches, tail tucked between his legs, waiting for a beating.

"I'm not angry, Alex. But you don't like to leave home—so what made you go?" For something to make him leave was bad enough, but to make him run close to two hundred miles meant he would have left this morning and in a hurry. And yes, a werewolf could cover that distance in that amount of time, but it should have nearly killed him. I looked him over. He wasn't sucked in and dehydrated; he was chirpy and fresh, ready to rumble.

He still wasn't answering. Talking to a werewolf could be like talking to a large child; the simplicity of the wolf's mind regressed the human's mind to a toddler's state if their will wasn't strong enough, which his definitely wasn't.

I changed tactics. Crouching down, I patted my leg. "Alex, come." He still cringed. I remembered my dropped pepperoni. Retrieving it, I tried again. "Alex, come here, see what I have? Pepperoni, it's one of your favorites." That did the trick. He bowled me over trying to get the pepperoni. "Wait! You can have it if you answer me." We were sprawled out on the floor together, Alex drooling all over my shirt, large canines dripping as he stared at the pepperoni I held just out of reach.

"How did you get here? Did you run all the way?" My change in questions brought a light to his eyes.

"No, no. Didn't run all way. Ran and jumped in noisy truck. Zoom down big road, jump out at other house. Wait for Ryleeeeeee!" He howled the end of my name and I shushed him. This wasn't a motel that catered to pets and I was pretty sure even with John's failing eyesight he wouldn't miss a two-hundred-pound werewolf if it kept up howling.

I handed Alex the pepperoni. I knew that the 'other house' was the motel. I had told him that sometimes I stayed at my 'other house' when it was too late to drive all the way home. 'Big road' was the highway and I suspected 'noisy truck' was a semi.

The second pepperoni stick appeared in my hand. "Can you answer another question for me?"

He nodded eagerly and gave a little yip of excitement. I shushed him, got up off the ground and shut the door. Well, propped it closed anyway.

I pulled a chair around, sat down and patted my knee. Alex scrambled over to me, placing his elongated muzzle on my lap. I scratched him behind his left ear and he whined with pleasure. "Okay, buddy. This is a hard question, maybe even scary. But you need to tell me and then you can have the pepperoni."

Amber eyes stared up at me, totally devoted, completely loyal. He whined again and a loud thumping of his tail let me know he was ready for the question.

"What scared you away from the house today? Was it the pack?" I continued to scratch his ears. Sure it was a dirty tool to distract him, but otherwise, we could be circling around the question for weeks before I found out what happened.

He tried to pull away, but I put the pepperoni on my lap right in front of his nose. "Just tell me what happened this morning and then you can have it." Ah, the old stick and carrot routine, it never failed.

Alex bared his teeth and said, "Pack came, chasing, biting. Wanting to kill. Safer to run than fight." He hung his head in shame with his last words.

"That's okay, buddy. I would've run too." I mulled over his words and absently gave him the pepperoni. The pack had been getting more aggressive the last few months. Alex had been with me almost seven months now, and at first I'd thought there would be nothing to worry about. Slowly, the pack had encroached more and more on my land, marking territory and making forays closer and closer to the house. A sigh escaped me and I scratched my head. Just add another problem onto the plate.

I knew from experience he wouldn't go home now without me. Thanks to all that was holy I had a collar for Alex that hid his true form from anyone who might be able to see it—once more thanks to Milly—so he could come with me for the next few days. Having him with me would make it a little more difficult to maneuver, but a lot less lonely.

Darkness fell, the sky clear and the stars easily visible. No sign of a thunderstorm, or any other bad weather for that matter. Stuffing Alex into the Jeep,

I said, "Stay here, buddy, I've got to get us a room change."

Once John saw the damage, he gave me the nicest room the motel had, a suite with two separate beds stuck in the sixties.

"Can't believe it," John said and handed me my new room key. "You think they were after you specific-like?"

"Nah, I wasn't even in there, John. I bet they were just looking for an easy score." I felt a bit guilty; after all, it was my werewolf that caused the damage. I'd leave an extra large tip in the morning.

I waved to John and quietly beckoned Alex to come once the manager was out of sight. Alex bounded from the Jeep and barreled past me into the suite, throwing himself onto the green shag carpet and rolling about with total abandon. "Listen, buddy, no more breaking into rooms, just wait by my Jeep, okay?"

Alex just stared at me, amber eyes uncomprehending. Letting out another sigh, I took off my jacket and placed my blades on the bed. My night-time routine never changed, no matter where I slept. The only thing I wouldn't do tonight, since Alex was here, was go for a run.

Going through combinations involving hands, feet, elbows, and knees, I worked a circle around an imaginary opponent. Muay Thai was my preferred method of hand-to-hand fighting; it gave me the most possibilities for striking out at someone. I always practiced in my working clothes, so that whatever restrictions they gave me, I learned to deal with before an actual fight. Fight like you practice and practice like you fight.

That was what my instructors drilled into me. Once I'd gone through the various blows, I dropped to the ground, first into a plank, then into push-ups; over to my back for crunches, and then back to a plank. Sweat dripped around me, my jeans sticking to my body, and I ignored it all. No matter what, I needed my body to be strong and fit for fighting. If it failed me, then I would fail a child, and that was not acceptable.

An hour and a half after I started, I finally let myself quit. Leaving Alex to guard the main room and front door, I headed into the bathroom to shower off. Taking advantage of someone else's hot water tank, I stayed in until the water cooled, my muscles tensing under the sudden temperature change. Stepping out onto the tile floor, water dripping everywhere, I glanced up at the foggy mirror. The heat from the shower sluiced off me as ice trailed down my spine. In bold letters written across the mirror were the words: *"Cross the Veil and Die."*

I snatched a towel and wrapped myself up in it, then searched the room, opening the two cupboards and the single closet. Nothing. I peeked out into the main room to see Alex sprawled out on the bed, but no one else. Closing the bathroom door, I used the only other towel in the room to wipe the mirror clean, my hands shaking just a little. The words seemed to be etched into the glass, and all my efforts at erasing them were futile. Giving up, I stepped out of the bathroom, preferring to dress in front of Alex, who had no concept of nudity, than in the room where it felt like someone was watching me. Give me blood and gore any day over perversion and peeping toms—probably creepy, greasy little men. Damn, someone already knew I was looking for India. The only person I'd told was Milly. Could she have spoken to the wrong person in the Coven? Shit.

Clean clothes on, hair towel-dried, I crawled into bed and patted the covers. Some people might think it weird that I let a werewolf sleep with me. But when you have immunity and can't be turned into a werewolf, there really is nothing to worry about. Other than the atrocious dog farts. He curled up at my feet, let loose one of said farts, and promptly began to snore.

Despite the words on the mirror, the worry over India and the pack chasing Alex away from home, sleep took me in less than ten minutes, my workout giving my body the tired edge it needed to drop off into dreamland.

Bad dreams were usual for me as my mind relived my past, and tried to make things better. I opened my eyes in my dream and it was Christmas morning, early, and Berget was tiptoeing into my room, not realizing my eyes were already open, her bright yellow pajamas and housecoat making her easy to see. She'd always had a thing for the neon shades.

"Rylee, it's Christmas morning! Wake up, we can go get our stockings!"

I closed my eyes. "This isn't real."

"What's not real?" I opened my eyes and stared into her pristine blue ones, and wondered if perhaps I was wrong, perhaps this was real and the rest of my life was just a bad dream. A nightmare.

She reached out her small hand, rubbed it against my cheek, brushed off a tear.

"Why are you crying, Rylee? Why are you sad? This is a happy day."

I brushed away another tear. "Berget, come here, let me hold you for a minute." She skipped away laughing.

"Silly, Rylee, you can't catch me!" Her face suddenly contorted. "Run! RUN!"

Her voice shattered what was left of the dream and I woke up, my breath coming in shallow gulps. The dream was nothing new and it would fade, leaving my adrenaline to also fade out in a matter of minutes. Or it would have, except for a shuffle of feet on the other side of my door and the faint jiggle of the handle, which caused my adrenaline to spike; I leapt out of bed.

Alex rumbled softly, his eyes half-closed. "Man with gun." I knew who that meant. It was O'Shea on the other side of the door.

If O'Shea thought he'd find me shaking in my boots, he was about to get another thing coming. I was about to use Milly's tactics to the hilt.

10

I stripped out of my clothes and ran to the door, trying not to think too hard about my desire to show off my body to O'Shea. With one last thought to precaution, I grabbed a blade with my left hand. Just in case.

Taking a deep breath I snatched the door open, holding the blade behind the door where it wouldn't be visible, and said, "Hello?" in my best sultry voice. Much to my embarrassment, there was no one at the door. I peeked around the corner. Nothing. Not a single movement.

Alex came to stand beside me, sniffing the air. I could have sworn I'd heard someone. A glance at Alex told me I hadn't been hearing things. His lips were curled back over his teeth and a steady growl slipped past his lips.

Pulling him back inside and putting some clothes on was my first prerogative. The second was to find out what Alex had smelled.

I crouched down to his level, dressed and with my blade attached, just in case. "What did you smell Alex? Was it a human? I thought it was 'man with a gun?'"

He shook his head and snorted once. "No! Yes!" He barked out. "Wolf, big leader wolf at door. But man with gun too."

Not entirely sure he was smelling right, thinking perhaps he was still spooked from his run in with the pack that morning, I did something I had never done before. I Tracked O'Shea. A moment of searching and I found him. Sure enough, he was close, but not close enough to be the perp at the door. I started to close the connection, but got a feeling of utter hopelessness that stopped me. It hurt me as if it were my own emotions, and not his that I was experiencing. My hands clenched into fists and I drew away from O'Shea, afraid I might feel sorry for him. It was one of the many reasons I didn't like Tracking anything but kids. Adults were far too complex; kids, for the most part, were simple.

Believing Alex, I got dressed, then bundled him into the Jeep and headed to the front desk to check out. Sure, it was four in the morning, but I wasn't going to be able to sleep, wondering who exactly was trying to break into my room. I might not be able to be turned into a werewolf, that didn't mean that they couldn't still rip me to shreds.

"Alex, stay." I raised my hand to him and then went to the back of the Jeep. Digging around in the back seat I found his collar. It was a simple, wide leather collar with two diamonds in the top. Yes, I said diamonds, and yes the collar had cost me a bundle, but it was worth it. The diamonds were part of the spell woven into the collar to keep people from seeing him for what he truly was.

Another pang centered around my heart. Milly was such a huge part of my life, how was I going to do all I needed to without her help? Again, I shook off those thoughts and fingered the collar. Once on Alex, all the average person saw was a very large black dog of indiscriminate breeding. Others, those who could see through the Veil, saw him for what he was, but most of them wouldn't point fingers for fear of being pointed at themselves.

Slipping the collar over his big head I said, "Now, while you're with me, you don't leave my side, not for an instant. Got it?"

Alex nodded and crossed his heart with a big claw. I laughed. Some days he seemed so human. It broke my heart a little to see him trapped like this, knowing there was no way out for him.

I shook off my melancholy and walked down to the office, Alex tight against my leg. He was very literal, which was always good to remember.

The office was quiet when I stepped in, the creak of the door the only noise. "Mary?" I called out. John should have been off his night shift by now, his wife Mary taking over in the early hours of the morning. There was no answer. I tried again. "John? Hello, anybody?"

A shuffle from behind the back door and Alex began to growl. I wrapped my hand through his collar. No need to make matters worse and have Alex making more werewolves.

Another shuffle, and the door opened. "Checking out, Ry? Kinda early, ain't it?" John wheezed out.

I blinked. "Yeah. You okay, John? You look like you've pulled an all nighter."

He blushed. "Maybe you of all people would be the one to believe me. I got a funny feeling near the end of my shift last night. Hairs I got left all stood up on end and I got the feeling like I needed to have all the lights on. Find a shotgun and protect the homestead. Weird, huh? I didn't like what I was feeling, so I told Mary to stay in bed and lock the door."

His description didn't really surprise me. Humans don't like the feeling those from the Veiled world give off, even though we all pretty much live side by side. It seemed Alex was right; it had been his pack leader. She was quite the bitch and the amount of power she carried around could make even the strongest heart stutter. She must have set old John's spidey senses into overdrive. His rheumy eyes looked up at me and then flicked down to the large black dog at my side.

Before he could ask, I cut him off. "This is my dog, Alex. He followed me here and I didn't have the heart to leave him out in the Jeep. If there's an extra charge or penalty for having him in the room . . ." I trailed off at the look John was giving Alex.

"Never seen a dog quite that big before. Seen a wolf once. 'Bout that size." He stared up at me, his mind behind the rheumy eyes far more shrewd than I gave him credit for.

It was my turn to blush. "I guess, if you say so." I pulled out two one-hundred dollar bills, more than twice what the room was worth for the night, and laid them on the counter. "Will that cover it?"

John smiled at me. "That's fine, Ry. You and your . . . dog . . . are always welcome here. He don't bite, do he?"

I shook my head. "No, of course not. I'd have to have him euthanized if he was to start that sort of thing." My hand tightened on the collar. Alex may be simple, but he wasn't stupid and he was very sensitive to the vibes people threw off. His tongue lolled and he kept his eyes lowered.

We left the motel, heading west on I-94, stopping only for breakfast at a McDonald's drive-thru, mostly for Alex. I ordered a coffee, black, and a breakfast sandwich to ease my hunger pangs. Alex had three sandwiches, a stack of hotcakes, and a large hot chocolate that he lapped up eagerly. There were still some very human things about him, despite his less-than-human exterior.

"Ready for a road trip, buddy?" My hands already on the wheel, my fingers licked clean of the fast food grease.

"Road trip!" Alex howled out the window, which set the dogs in the area into a frenzy.

"Back in the Jeep," I said as I leaned over and rolled the window up. He slumped in his seat and gave me his best hound dog eyes.

I let out a sigh. "At least wait till we get on the interstate. Then you can howl out the window all you like. All right?"

His eyes lit up and his tongue lolled out past his wicked sharp teeth. I laughed at him and hit the gas as I drove up the on ramp. At least this trip would be anything but boring.

If only I knew how true that would turn out to be.

11

It was his day off. He should have been relaxing at home, not rehashing a case, but he couldn't settle himself down. For some reason, Adamson's digs still stung. It didn't help that he *knew* she was out there hunting for India. Picking up a sheaf of papers he had on his retro black-and-white kitchen table, he flipped through the pictures.

India, the missing girl, showed a distinct resemblance to a young Adamson. He put the two pictures side by side; although Adamson was in her teens when her picture was taken, they looked close enough to be sisters, and *that* was a little spooky. Both of them had auburn hair that fell in waves, and there was a softness to both sets of eyes that got under his skin, made him feel like a big bastard.

With a sudden jerk, he threw the papers back on the table and let out a sharp gust of air. He never had trouble controlling his temper, but something about Adamson set him off, and she reveled in poking at him. Like it had become an Olympic Sport for her.

He fingered the tracking device he'd brought home with him, thinking maybe he'd drive out past her place, but the thing had flicked off like it was wont to do. No amount of changing batteries, updating software, or switching out parts made a difference. He'd learned it would come back on line when it felt damn good and ready, and not a bloody second before.

Reaching into the fridge, he pulled out a beer, paused and then put it back. Just in case he got a hit on the tracker.

Sitting back at the table, he spread the file out, flipping through it a page at a time. The similarities in the cases Adamson managed to pull out of her hat on her own were more than a little suspicious. The kids would go missing without a trace, local law enforcement could do nothing, somehow the parents would track Adamson down, and they would pay her to find the kids. And on all the cases she'd been brought in on, she'd found the kids, though not always alive.

And there was the rub. She had a better rate of success than any FBI agent, than the whole freaking agency! He slammed a fist onto the table and the tracking device lit up, blinking softly.

Grabbing it, he smiled. She was heading south. This wasn't the first time and the pattern was too obvious; someone in New Mexico was helping her, and it was time O'Shea met up with them both and had a chat with them.

Grabbing his jacket and keys, he jogged out to his vehicle. The wind was picking up and it whistled through the alley alongside his house. With a couple of days off in a row, it was a good time for a road trip, and this way no one would be the wiser to his deviation from procedure.

The drive to New Mexico was uneventful. I sped like crazy, trying to catch time I didn't have in the first place. I could feel India, feel her fear and confusion and, worse than that, her strength slipping away from her. Not like she was dying, but that her willpower was slowly being eaten away. Whoever had her was making a push to get her under their control. I couldn't help but wonder if that was what happened to Berget. The two cases were too damn similar for my liking. The park, the time of day, the damn date—even down to the swing India had been on. The only difference I could see was Berget wasn't a spirit seeker, which was what I thought India was. My hands were wet on the steering wheel from my sweat, as I continued to roll the two cases over in my mind. My lower back felt clammy, and I feared the worst. That this case would end the same way Berget's had—in a death where I couldn't even bring the body back to her parents for closure.

I shook the thought away. No, I wouldn't go there. Guilt rolled over me. I'd been so young, both in age and ability, that when Berget had been snatched, I didn't know what I was doing. Still, I felt like it was my fault she was snatched, that I was somehow responsible for her going missing. It wasn't hard for the detectives on the case to decide I was guilty, not when I tended to agree with them.

"This time will be different," I said, startling Alex out of a light doze. He cocked his head at me, then closed his eyes and went back to sleep.

After what was etched into my bathroom mirror, I knew they, whoever they were, knew I was coming for her. They also knew all about Berget, so I had to be ready to face whatever they would throw my way. None of this was making me feel better, not one bit.

Going as fast as I dared, only taking a short four-hour nap when I could no longer keep my eyes open, I cut our driving time by an hour and a half, getting us into Roswell by 4:30 in morning the next day. Or at least into the north side of the town.

Despite the town's reputation for UFO's because of that one singular crash, there was actually very little supernatural activity in the area—unlike North Dakota, which had more than its fair share of the weird and the wild. There was only one place I would stay while in Roswell, and it was run by a very large ogre who wore a ring similar in make to Alex's collar. In other words, he passed for human.

The Landing Pad, an apt name for the area, was a small motel with an attached bar catering to those needing to be discreet.

I parked and Alex followed me out, tight on my heels, my command that he stay close still with him. I stretched and he mimicked me as best as his contorted body would let him. It brought a smile to my face and I was glad he'd come to find me at the hotel, though the reason for it sucked.

The lady at the front desk checked me in, gave me a key and we went to our room. No point in calling in on my friend now, he slept till after noon every day. The Shaman I was here to see was even worse, she would be inactive until dusk. And if there was one thing I'd learned, it was that you didn't mess with a Shaman's schedule, not if you wanted their help.

Double locking the door behind me, I checked the room, and then flopped onto the bed, Alex throwing himself down beside me. Within moments I was asleep. For once, it was dreamless.

Hours later I pulled myself awake. "Damn," I flicked open the curtain. I'd slept longer than I'd planned. Jumping out of bed, I grabbed Alex and we headed out to find my friend. Ogre he might be, but he was also the best source of information I knew down here.

The motel's door barely creaked under my hand, but a voice still called to us from within the building.

"Won't be a second."

Knowing who it was, I followed where the voice had come from. A large, pale blue-skinned ogre stood in front of the stove, his dark blue hair in a long braid down his back. He wasn't as big as some I'd seen, but he was still large, well over seven feet. He had piercings through his nose, lip, and eyebrow, but none in his ears. Absently I wondered if it signified anything or if he was just trying to keep up with the human culture.

I sauntered up to him, sure of my welcome. "How you doing, Dox?"

With a roar, he spun and pulled me into a bear hug, slapping my back, much to Alex's displeasure as made apparent by his muttered grumbling.

"I'll be snookered, Rylee! It's been months since you been down our way. How in freaky fairyland are you?" He held me at arm's length, ignoring Alex's grumbles, and inspected my condition. I must not have passed because before I could answer, he spun me around and sat me at the large table. I always felt like a child sitting at a table that was made for Dox and his buddies. "Here, sit and eat." He pushed a plate of brownies toward me and I snagged one. If Dox was a perfectionist for anything, it was his baking. He smiled at me, a twinkle in his eye, "Freshly baked boggart brownies are the best for what ails you."

I froze with one of said brownies halfway to my mouth. "No boggarts in them I hope." He laughed at my expression and pushed one toward Alex, who sat at my side, a skeptical look on his face as he sniffed the pastry.

"Nah. Picked the recipe up from a boggart passing through and added it to my repertoire." He placed one big hand over his heart. "You wouldn't truly believe I'd feed you boggart without telling you, would you?"

I snorted. "I seem to remember a certain meal that consisted of mystery meat which turned out to be—"

"Ah yes, I remember. Let's not discuss that. It didn't turn out well for anyone." He grimaced and I smiled around the brownie. Goblin meat is not very tasty, no matter how many spices you add to it. And when the process reverses and the meat comes out the way it went in, it burns. I'd eaten nothing for the next week that didn't hurt all the way down.

"So, you here needing help?"

I nodded, my mouth full. He handed me a glass of milk. After a chug of moo juice, I answered him. "There's a kid I can't track and there was no evidence of her even being taken. Figured a shaman was my best bet. I was hoping Louisa would help me out."

Dox frowned and sat down across from me. "You haven't heard then?"

I frowned right back at him. "Haven't heard what?"

He let out a sigh and folded his hands on the table. "All the shamans, all except one, have left. Gone. Pfft." He made a flapping gesture with one big mitt.

"What? Louisa would never leave, this is her home!"

"I know, but she's gone. Not a word about it either until someone went looking and found only this Doran fellow."

My eyes widened. "A male shaman? That's taboo 'round here, isn't it?"

Dox nodded and pushed another brownie toward Alex, who took the square eagerly. "Yup. But he's all we've got now. Suppose you want to know where to go looking for the new guy?"

I stood up and brushed crumbs off my lap. "Yes, doubly so now."

Dox looked up at me, his eyes solemn. "Thought you didn't Track adults."

"Not going to Track them, Dox, just going to ask a few questions. If I have to work with this Doran, then fine. But I'd rather work with someone I know and can trust like Louisa."

"Well then." Dox stood and led me out of his kitchen, Alex right behind us. "Here's his address." He handed me a business card.

My eyebrows climbed near into my hairline. "He's handing out business cards?"

Dox smiled down at me and patted my head. "Wait till you meet him, Rylee. I'm betting you two are going to just" —he clapped his hands together— "hit it off." It was the twinkle in his eye that told me this Doran would be trouble. But I went anyway. I needed him to help me find India, no matter how much trouble he was going to be.

12

Alex was not happy I left him with Dox while I went on without him to meet with Doran. He whined and cried, whimpered, and finally started howling. I felt awful, knowing how submissive and downright needy he was. That is, until Dox pulled out another pan of boggart brownies, and Alex suddenly forgot all about me.

I pulled out of the driveway. I was headed to Shawnee road, on the far east side of town. Dusk fell and shadows darkened the road as I pulled up to where Doran was supposed to be. Sitting in my Jeep, I looked out over the empty lot. At first glance, it was nothing more than an overgrown weed garden, one lone attempt at a cactus in the far right corner, miserable excuses for houses on either side of the mid-sized lot, and no actual house of any sort. I glanced at the realtor posting out front and checked it against what Dox had given me. It matched up. Which could only mean one thing.

I focused on my second sight, narrowing my eyes, and saw the flicker of the Veil cross my vision. When I opened my eyes fully, there was a massive adobe house with a beautiful herb garden, two small fountains in the shape of fish spouting water out their mouths and into a pond with koi swimming lazily about. Swanky for this part of town, even if it was on the other side of the Veil.

"How the hell did you manage this?" I asked no one in particular. Which is why I was startled to get an answer.

"Hard work. A little luck. Good timing."

I started as a body materialized behind the voice and a young man, no older than myself, was suddenly sitting on the passenger seat. Good thing indeed I hadn't brought Alex with me. Doran was an average build. It was hard to distinguish his height while sitting, but I guessed he was about my height. White blond hair stuck straight up as if magnetized, the tips dyed black. It was a sharp contrast for his dark green eyes that spoke of humor and fun, not magic and wisdom. Two piercings over his left eyebrow and one in the right side of his lower lip made him look a bit like a punk rocker. I had a very hard time seeing him as a shaman.

I composed myself as fast as I could. "You must be Doran."

He smiled, a big open grin splitting his face from ear to ear. "Yes. And those beautiful eyes must make you Rylee."

I blinked, not sure how to react. Most people didn't like my eyes, too many colors to be normal.

Clearing my throat, I nodded. "I need help with tracing a kid on the other side of the Veil, but I don't know how deep she's been taken or which entry point to use."

Doran shrugged. "Which one? Isn't that always the question?"" For a price, of course." His eyes darkened. "The deep levels on the other side of the Veil are not very welcoming right now. Perhaps you'd be better off forgetting about this kid."

Deep levels? What was he talking about? I didn't ask, though, as I knew it would only cost more and it likely didn't matter.

"How much?" I chose to ignore his warning. Shamans were like that, always full of doom and gloom, and in that at least, he was no different.

"The price is steep, I'm not sure you will be willing to pay it." He lifted an eyebrow, the two rings catching the last of the light from the setting sun through the windshield. "Come in, it's far more cozy in my home."

Leaving the safety and additional weapons in my Jeep, I followed him into his territory after a quick glance around to be sure no one was looking. A shiver of air rippled around me as I stepped across the Veil. It was what separated the human world from the worlds where many of the supernatural creatures lived, hiding out just under the human's noses.

Anyone watching would have seen us disappear and, though I was nervous, Doran didn't seemed to be bothered at all. I knew most humans, if they did see something, would shake it off as a trick of the light. That's not to say some humans didn't go looking for the supernatural; they just didn't know what they were looking at most of the time.

The fountain splashed merrily and the koi swam to the surface as we passed. "Little beggars," Doran muttered, tossing them some small crumbs from his pocket. They gulped at the pieces, their mouths opening wide and showing flashes of silver and gold as they jostled for the bits of food.

Inside the adobe house, the air was warm, and a large open fire pit in the middle of the structure roared upward, keeping the chill autumn air at bay.

"Sit, we will discuss your needs . . . and mine," he said, motioning to a plush cushion on the edge of the fire.

A worm of unease began to crawl through the base of my spine, making its way upward. I didn't know this shaman and I'd walked in here like it was safe. What had I been thinking? "I'll stand. You know what I need, name your price."

Doran stared at me across the flames, his gaze travelling the length of my body twice before resting on my face. Slowly, he smiled. "Perhaps you can guess at my price for the knowledge you seek."

For the second time that day I blushed, the heat from the flames was nothing compared to the heat in my face. My jaw clenched at what he was implying. "I think you'd better just spit it out. I don't like guessing games."

He grinned at me, white teeth almost sparkling. My eyes narrowed; I didn't like this, but he was the only chance I had at finding India in time. Almost without thinking, I reached for her and was surprised when she reached back, just the faintest brush of her mind at the very edges of my own.

"Help, please."

Stunned, I saw Doran's mouth moving but heard nothing. Not one kid had ever reached for me, had ever felt I was going to try and help them. "I'm coming, just hang on," I whispered under my breath, not sure if I could speak to her mind to mind.

"What was that?"

I waved my hand at him to continue and tried to piece together what he'd already said.

"You see, I have some very particular needs," he said, a smile tipping up the corners of his mouth. "I have very refined tastes, and quite frankly, the people around here just aren't satisfying them."

Jaw tight, I held very still. It was the first time I'd ever dealt with a male shaman. I didn't know if he was bluffing or if he truly wanted to get in my pants. "I'm not that kind of girl." I bit out.

"Not even to save a child? A little girl?" Doran spread his hands across his knees and rubbed his thighs. "Isn't she about the same age as your sister was when she went missing?"

Ice formed around my spine and heart. Maybe he thought I'd buckle under the mention of my lost family. "No, actually. Berget was younger by a few years." Stepping around the fire I leaned down until our noses almost touched. "Try to use her for bait again, Doran, and it will be you that will go missing next." By the end, my words were a bare whisper, only just audible above the crackle of the fire.

"Oh, Rylee, how I wish I'd met you years ago." He whispered back, as if I hadn't just threatened his life. "A pint of blood will do, I suppose. Though I'd much prefer it to be taken by my mouth, I suspect you'll insist on a blade?"

I snapped backwards as if he'd slapped me. Blood. If he wanted blood, then . . . "You're a daywalker?"

Steepling his fingers under his chin, he laughed softly. "What did you think? That any old shaman could step in and replace all those women?"

Daywalker. Vampire. They were the same thing, only one roamed the night, and the other roamed the day. Why hadn't Dox warned me about this? Likely he didn't know.

I started to sweat, old fears surfacing. I'd faced down a daywalker once, to save a child. The end result was the daywalker was dead, and the kid safe, but I still had nightmares. Not to mention a few deep tissue scars that would never fade. The one in my lower back, just above my tailbone, started to throb as if I'd poked it. The daywalker had tackled me from behind, almost wrapping his teeth around my lower spine. If Milly hadn't been with me on that search, I'd have been killed. What Doran had just said caught up with me.

"Speaking of those missing women, where are they?" I forced the fear back down my throat.

Doran tipped his head to one side. "You don't hunt for adults, Rylee, so why would you care what happened to them?"

"It's important to a friend. He wants to know." I fingered the handle of my blade. "And since you took their places, you should know what happened."

"I do, but if you want that information, you're going to have to give me more than blood. I want you bound to me."

Nope, no one was worth that, not even the shamans I'd come to count as allies. In fact, I wasn't so sure I'd bind myself to him even for a kid. I shook my head.

"Whatever, I'm not looking for the shamans." I cracked my knuckles, nerves starting to show through my tough girl exterior. "I guess you can't help me then, especially not if it's one of your own that took the girl." I started to back away from him. No fucking way I was turning my back on him now.

"Oh, I can help you, Rylee. Besides, it wasn't one of mine who stole the girl, I can tell you that much." He paused and took a long slow breath as if tasting the air. "You see, I just want a taste of the good stuff. The blood all the daywalkers and vamps sing about when we get together for our yearly convention." His eyes, they were full of laughter. He was having fun with this, teasing me.

"Only one blood sucker has ever bitten me, and he's no more," I said, sure of myself.

Of course, he blew that out of the water with what he said next.

"Rylee, Rylee. You don't understand." Laughing, he stood and started toward me. For each step he took, I stepped back. "All of us blood suckers, as you call us, are connected by the same blood. So when he bit you"—he reached out for me and I batted his hand away—"we all knew just how delicious you were. It's what got him killed. He was so caught up in *your* blood singing through his veins, he didn't recognize the danger of having a witch behind him."

The door bumped against my back. I twisted the handle, but it was slippery under my sweaty fingers, making it impossible to turn.

Doran lunged forward, pinning my body to the door with his own. "I won't hurt you, Rylee, I promise, you will like the bite I give you."

Nope, not doing this again.

Kicking out, I caught him just below the knee. The bone crunched under my foot; he screamed and I caught a glimpse of fangs. Spinning out of his reach, I put the fire between us. The worst part of this was that I couldn't just leave. I needed him to give me an entry point into the other side of the Veil. I pulled my blade, holding it at the ready, eyes narrowed, ready to do what damage I had to without killing him.

Doran limped toward me, a grimace on his face. "I don't have time for this. I forgot how damn touchy your type are."

My ears perked up. "You aren't going to try that again?"

With a grunt he slid into a heavily cushioned chair. "Joints are the hardest thing to heal. They are never a clean break and take a lot of energy to put the pieces back together."

"Why would you tell me that?"

"I get the feeling you might need the info when you go after this girl," he said, his hand rubbing his knee.

Hmm. Interesting. And what had he meant by my type? Like blood type? Or that I was a Tracker and an Immune?

"Let's keep this simple, Rylee. I want your blood. I'd love to sink my fangs in you . . . amongst other things." His gaze held mine and a burst of heat whipped through me. Damn, he was good if he could rile me up even after freaking the hell out of me.

"Don't even think it," I said, tearing my eyes from his.

"I will settle for you donating into a cup for me." He pointed at a table across the room. Sitting there, as if he'd known I wouldn't go for the whole 'bite me, do me' routine, was a crystal flower vase with a straight razor beside it.

Swallowing hard, I let out a sharp puff of air. "Okay. But I will fill it half up. Then, you will tell me my entry point, and I will fill it the rest of the way."

Winking at me, he settled deeper into the chair, one hand massaging the knee I'd busted. Stupid daywalker, my fear was giving way to anger.

The crystal vase sparkled in the light, sending rainbows of color skittering across the table. Pretty.

Rolling up my left sleeve, I ignored the razor he'd laid out for me and pulled a knife out of my boot. It was clean, sharper than the razor and, better than both those things, I knew it had no added substances on it. Like a drug that would knock me out and leave me vulnerable to Doran's fangs.

With a swift slice, I cut across my arm, deep enough that I didn't feel it at first. The blood welled in the groove I'd cut; I placed it over the vase, and then I felt the first sting. With every ounce of my self-control, I kept my arm dripping into the crystal vase while keeping an eye on Doran. At the halfway mark, I nodded at him. Holding the knife cut shut, I moved my arm away from the vase.

"Okay, spill," I said. My arm dripped blood on the floor; somehow I knew that would drive Doran nuts, the wasting of 'good blood.' I was right.

He started to splutter and stood up. "Put your arm back over the vase."

"Tell me my entry point." I felt the distinct shift of power move from him to me.

His eyes dilated and his mouth hung slightly open, fangs extending, like a junkie staring at his next fix. No response.

I let go of the cut and let the blood drip to the floor, then scuffed it with my boot. "I can let the next half pint fall to the floor and technically, I've fulfilled the bargain."

Licking his lips, he gestured with his hand, waving me back to the vase. "A mineshaft. You'll find the closest entry point to her in a mineshaft."

Well, that only narrowed my search down a bit. Coal was plentiful in North Dakota, and along with that came a lot of mineshafts. Some known, some not so known.

"No other details?" I squeezed out another few drops onto the floor. It hurt, but his response was worth it.

"Stop! Okay, put your arm over the damn vase, Tracker," he snapped, his eyes glittering with anger.

"You're going to actually help me? Rather than just give vague answers?"

Nodding emphatically, he again gestured. "Just stop wasting that blood."

Placing my arm back over the vase, I let the blood run. With every pump of my heart, a gentle flow slid out. I'd cut deep, but not into an artery or it'd be spurting blood—though I was going to have to make a side trip to the hospital for stitches after this.

Doran came to stand behind me, his body close enough that I could feel the heat off his body. Unlike their counterparts whose skin was cool and tended to be clammy, daywalkers ran hot. Not that I knew that from a personal introduction; I'd never had to deal with a true vampire. They were rare, deadly, and didn't tend to leave their territories. Not to mention daywalkers were weaker, more human, and less badass blood suckers.

"The mineshaft, it runs deep, over two hundred feet straight down, and it's back in your home territory." He took a deep breath and my hair actually fluttered toward him. With his chin just above my shoulder, he whispered into my ear. "They stole her, in the light of day, underneath her mother's watchful eye. One moment she was in the playground, then poof" —he blew across my ear, sending a course of shivers through me— "she was gone."

Just like Berget.

He stepped back, leaving me to listen to my heart hammering in my chest, the beat of it loud enough that I knew he could see my pulse jumping in my throat. Fear. I told myself it was fear and adrenaline; that was all.

Doran smiled at me, just lifting one corner of his mouth. He grabbed the lip rings with his fang and pulled at them, capturing my gaze with ease. There, at the corner of his mouth, it looked soft, as if it were the perfect place to press my lips to his.

"Your half pint is finished, Rylee."

"Huh." I cleared my throat. "Right."

"Here," he said, that wicked smile still lingering on his lips, "Let me help you. I am rather good at stitching up wounds."

I stumbled away from him, more out of fear for what I was feeling than for my safety. "No. You have

your blood and I have my information." He was trying to pull me under his thrall, and I was falling for it,
my mind weak from the blood loss.

Keeping my eyes on him, I again backed toward
the door, gripping my arm, keeping it closed as best
I could. I had bandages in the Jeep. I just had to get
there.

13

I was shaking by the time I got to my Jeep, and I knew I'd lost more blood than the pint I'd had to give up. "Ah, damn it!" I couldn't get the wrap tight enough on my forearm. Giving up, I tied off the wrap and turned on the Jeep. The engine turned over nicely and I pulled away from the curb.

If I'd been home, I would've gone to the hospital and checked on Giselle, and got stitched up there. As it was, Dox could stitch me up.

I barely made it back to the Landing Pad when a wave of dizziness crashed over me. Leaning on the horn, I didn't lift off until Dox came running out, Alex on his heels with a grin stretched across his face.

"What the hell happened?" Dox's voice rebounded as if he had a megaphone. Just another quirk of being an ogre. A perk when you had to yell over a noisy crowd; a serious pain when it was right in your ear.

"A bargain. I got what I needed, but now I'm thinking I could use some stitches."

Dox helped me out and, when my legs buckled, swept me up into his arms and strode into his bar. "Seriously, I didn't think he'd go this far. I'll kill him."

"Can't. He's a daywalker."

He stopped mid-stride and looked down at me. "Did he bite you?"

I shook my head. "No, but I had to give him some blood." I took a deep breath. "Just a little." I tried to make a pinching motion with my thumb and forefinger on the hand of the arm I'd cut. Nothing moved. "Oops."

"Oops, my ass, Rylee. You cut too damn deep!" He laid me out on the bar. The polished wood was cool and felt nice against my bare skin. Bare skin?

Lifting my head, I glanced down at my body. Apparently I'd passed out somewhere in the process as my shirt had been cut off me. Hell, I'd liked that shirt.

Dox was on the inside of the bar, my arm in his hands as he cleaned and probed the knife wound. "Why did you use your own blade? You know they are spelled to cut deep."

Shrugging while lying down didn't really give the effect I wanted. "I didn't want to use the razor he left out. Was afraid he might have put something on it."

He grunted, but stopped chastising me. We both knew daywalkers, just like their counterparts, were more than apt when it came to knocking out their victims and draining them dry over a long period of time.

At first the tug and pull on my skin as Dox stitched me up didn't hurt. It just felt weird. And then all my adrenaline started to wear off.

"Ow! Damn it." I tried to keep myself from jerking away from him. Alex bounded over to me, bunting his head into my good hand, which hung off the bar. "Hey, buddy." His tongue lolled and his eyes were wide with worry. "Rylee hurt."

"Only for a minute. Were the brownies good?" I made a real attempt to not give into the pain starting to burn up my arm.

Alex bobbed his head. "More brownies?"

"Maybe later."

Dox stuck me again and I hissed in a breath past my teeth. "Unnecessary roughness."

"Where's Milly?" The ogre asked.

"The Coven finally accepted her. It meant she had to cut ties with me and Giselle." A new pain flared up, right around my heart.

He paused in his of torturing me. "And she did it? Are you kidding me?"

Again, I attempted a shrug. "It's what she's wanted as long as I've known her. I'm not going to take it away from her. Though I still want to kick her ass."

The stitching resumed and I kept my other hand busy petting Alex's head, scratching his ears, reminding myself this was the price to pay for India. That helped.

"I have to drive home as soon as possible," I said as Dox put in the last stitch. I looked over at his needle-work. "Those are good, better than any doctor I've seen do stitches."

He snorted out a laugh. "You don't get to the top of the food chain without being able to stitch yourself up from time to time."

It took me a minute to realize what he meant. "You've had to stitch yourself up?"

"More than once." He held his hand out to me and helped me to sit up on the bar, just as the door binged and the first real patron of the day came in.

Just my luck, it was someone I knew, far too well.

O'Shea.

"Adamson, what the hell are you . . . are you bleeding?" His voice shifted, as he covered the distance between us. I'll be buggered; he was worried about me.

"Yes, thank you very much. Now if you wouldn't mind, I'm half naked and would like to get some clothes on without you staring at all that God gave me." I glanced sideways at him and batted my eyelashes for good measure.

Even in the dim light, I watched in fascination as the color crept up his neck and into his face. "Are you blushing, O'Shea?" *Milly, Milly, why didn't I believe you about this power women have over men long ago?*

"Don't tease him, Rylee. Any man would stare at what you've got." Dox gave me a long wink; I knew he didn't mean anything by it. I stretched my arms over my head, feeling O'Shea's gaze linger on my skin, like a touch. If this was all it took to keep him quiet, then I needed to modify my regular wardrobe to be more like Milly, with skin-tight, revealing clothes. Anything to keep O'Shea off balance.

"I'm not staring at you. I'm looking to see where all the blood came from. Or is it not yours?" His voice prickled with malice.

I froze with my hands above my head. "You want me to leave them up here while you read me my rights?" Shimmying off the bar, I hopped to the floor, not lowering my hands. The world swayed and all thoughts of bravado left me as I concentrated on not falling flat on my face.

Hands steadied me. "I guess that answers my question." O'Shea's voice rumbled too close for comfort. With a jerk, I slid out of his hands and backed up to the closest bar stool.

"What do you want?" I snapped, no longer interested in playing games.

"You mean to tell me that you don't know? Adamson, I'd have thought after all these years you'd know I frequent the dives of New Mexico on my off days." He pulled out a bar stool next to me and sat down.

"Beer," was all he said when Dox lifted his eyebrows. Of course, O'Shea couldn't see what Dox really was, anymore than he could see a werewolf and not a large dog slinking toward him with his teeth bared.

"Alex, here," I said, my tone brooking no argument. Alex grumbled under his breath, something that could easily be written off by human ears as a growl.

Pressing up against my leg, he glared at O'Shea, who turned to look at the "dog" at my side. "What is he?"

"A mutt," was my only answer. Dox put a coaster down in front of O'Shea, followed by an ice-cold beer that soaked through the paper coaster within seconds.

O'Shea nodded his thanks and took a long drag off the bottle. "Best beer I've tasted in a long while, almost a hint of something in it. Can't quite put my finger on it."

What the hell was this small chat shit? What was his game? As he and Dox discussed the different local brews, I slipped from my stool and headed to the back room where I knew Dox kept some spare clothes.

A black t-shirt that was a little on the tight side and said "Suck it!" on the front was not my first choice, but the other option was an extra large that stated it was a tool shed. Nope, "Suck it!" didn't look too bad, especially not with O'Shea waiting out front.

Alex stayed at my side, his presence a steady comfort. If I wasn't careful, I'd come to rely on him to be there, like a large teddy bear. I washed the blood off my arm and body then tugged the too-tight shirt on over my head.

Stepping into the bar again, I was shocked to see O'Shea passed out on the bar.

"What happened? I was only gone like five minutes." I plucked open one of O'Shea's eyelids.

Dox laughed. "Well, after he dissed my place—again—I offered him some of the local juice."

I let out a groan. "Ogre beer?"

He just smiled, didn't even bother to nod. "Well, how long will he be out?" The stuff was potent. What moonshine was to water, ogre beer was to human alcohol. I'd never tried it myself, though apparently it was sweet and tangy. It was the after kick that worried me.

"Oh, he'll be out for about an hour, then have a hangover for at least another four," Dox said, wiping down the bar around the FBI agent. And just where was his partner exactly? Nope, didn't matter, wasn't my issue.

"I've gotta go then. If I can get a head start, maybe I can keep him out of the way this time."

Dox walked me to the door. "He's the one who went after you, isn't he?"

Blinking away sudden tears, I cleared my throat and hid the moisture in my eyes with a hand through the hair. "Yeah, but he never could prove anything; not a motive, nothing. He just wanted to be right, to break the big case."

"Well, I'll stall him much as I can." He pulled me into a big hug, being careful of my arm, letting me go just as carefully.

A cold nose bumped into my hand. "Alex too."

Laughing, Dox lifted Alex into a hug, which the werewolf did his best to reciprocate—not an easy task when your limbs are stuck between human and wolf.

"Can't say I've ever hugged a werewolf before," Dox said, patting Alex on the head. The werewolf's tongue lolled out as he stared up at Dox. A sudden thought hit me—hard.

"If something ever happens to me, Dox, will you take Alex? His pack'll kill him."

The ogre frowned, his piercings clinking together. "I don't know, Rylee. Just don't get yourself into trouble, how about that?"

I nodded and pushed through the door into the brilliant white sunlight that was New Mexico. If only it were as easy as Dox made it out to be. The thing was, when it came to me and trouble, we went together like ice cream and pie.

14

The drive back to North Dakota took about the same amount of time as heading south, only now I was counting down in my head the time we had until O'Shea would be up and at 'em. Or more accurate, up and at me.

First thing, we went to the hospital. I didn't go in to see Giselle, just had the nurse give me the update. They didn't think she had swine flu—which I already knew—and she was being evaluated for a respite home.

"How soon will they know?"

The nurse flipped through the paperwork. "Looks like we should have everything back by the end of the week."

Tapping the counter I bit the edge of my lip. "You'll keep her in until then?"

"Yes, we don't get the final results back from her blood work until then either." The nurse said as a beeper went off. "Excuse me."

At the mention of blood, I fingered the stitches on my arm wrapped with a soft bandage.

Climbing back into my Jeep, I turned around and headed home to stock up on supplies. I would need flashlights, my climbing harness and rope, and riot gear, to name a few things. Almost three hours later, the place I called home came into sight.

As we pulled into the driveway, I reached for India and felt a distant pang of loneliness and fear, then a wash of curiosity. That was odd, and not in a good way. If whoever had her was piquing her curiosity, it might be harder to extricate her from them.

The big, two-story farmhouse needed a paint job, and there were parts of the white picket fence that were down, but it was still a sturdy house that more than did the job. Upstairs was all bedrooms, and I left that to Alex for the most part. My room was on the main floor with the kitchen off one side and the only bathroom in the house on the other.

The house was cool inside, a breeze blowing through the open windows, keeping the air from going stagnant while I was gone.

Alex whimpered and clung to my leg. Not a good sign. Waving for him to stay behind, then pressing one finger to my lips for him to stay quiet, I eased two blades out of my boots. The thing was, weapons, guns in particular, didn't always work around the supernatural. They would misfire, explode, and even fall apart for no apparent reason. Knives and blades on the other hand, they always worked just fine.

Creeping through the house, my ears strained to catch the slightest sound, a breath of air, the shuffle of clothing. The wooden floors didn't creak under my steps, but still the tension around me rose. Someone—or something—was in the house. I just didn't know what.

Looking over my shoulder at Alex, I lifted my eyebrows and pointed up. He nodded.

Whoever or whatever it was, they were upstairs. Damn. Moving as fast as I could while still staying quiet, I started up the curling staircase. I avoided the fourth step up; I knew it creaked. Just before the bend in the stairs that would expose me to the top floor, I paused.

Skin tingling, I knew I was in trouble a split second before the wash of magic hit me. Electricity danced over my body, blue and sparking as the spell slammed me into the far wall, and then it dissipated. Round one to Rylee and her magic dissolving abilities. At least I didn't get the full brunt of the spell.

"Alex, run!" was all I managed to gasp out before being slammed again, this time with a chair launched at me by another spell. It rarely took the bad guys long to realize they could use other things to smash me rather than using the magic itself. My head snapped against the plaster wall with a solid thud. Black circles spun across my vision; I tried to sit up and failed on the first attempt. Leaning against the wall, I used my legs to push me up. Alex leapt over me, growling and snarling, his hackles standing on end from the base of his neck all the way down his bushy tail.

Steps scampered down the stairs, the intruders no longer making any attempt to hide themselves.

"Alex." I moaned, grabbing at his collar. "Outside. Now."

My fingers tightened on the collar as the werewolf spun and scrambled back down the stairs and out the open front door, dragging me with him. The porch stairs bounced me hard as he ran full tilt out into the closest field.

Wheat stalks waved above my head as Alex ran, my body flopping limply, hitting every protruding rock that crossed our path. Damn, I was going to be bruised tomorrow. Of course, that was assuming whoever was trying to kill me would give up and go away.

A flash of blue ripped over our heads. Apparently they, whoever they were, were not going away just yet.

"Alex stop," I said. We couldn't just keep running. He skidded to a panting, shaking stop, his sides trembling with fear more than exhaustion. As a werewolf, he had more than enough strength to drag me around.

I lay there on the dirt, my mind racing with options. There just weren't that many. Rolling over to my belly, I began to army crawl deeper into the wheat patch. Alex crouched down and mimicked me, his claws digging into the soft, dry dirt.

If we could get around to the back of the house, I had weapons there stashed in the cellar. In particular, a water gun of sorts that worked off of a pump action that I could load with salt water—salt water worked wonders on magic users, blocking their ability to spell. I only had my two blades on me; I'd been stupid to try and face whoever was in the house without more.

Halfway through the wheat, I closed in on the back of the house, when a wisp of smoke curled past my nose. Alex whimpered. A crackle of the fire they'd lit reached my ears, just as I saw the first sign of flames curling toward us.

"Mother fuckers," I hissed. No choice now. I jumped to my feet, fought the first wave of vertigo and sprinted across the last hundred feet to the back of the house, Alex tight on my heels.

A bolt of blue electricity propelling a rock clipped my heel as I dove for cover, spinning me in the air. Hitting the ground hard knocked the wind out of me, but I didn't slow down; I couldn't, not if I wanted to make it out of this alive.

The wind blew hard, fanning the flames right toward the house at a speed I wasn't sure I could beat. Ripping open the cellar door, I pushed Alex down ahead of me and slammed the door shut, barring it behind us.

"Damn it all to hell," I grumbled under my breath, like it was a normal occurrence for me to be attacked in my own home. Because it wasn't, and the whole thing was freaking the hell out of me. Worse, if I let on how scared I was, I'd have Alex spazzing out in a split second. Let me tell you, having a panicked werewolf in a tight confined space is not a good idea, even if you are Immune.

I flipped on the light switch and the fluorescent bulb buzzed to life. The cellar door would buy us time—if we were lucky, about ten seconds before they blew it off its hinges.

I grabbed a flak jacket; it was thin, the lightest one on the market, to make it easy for me to hide it under my clothes. It wouldn't stop the spells, but it would help protect my body, which right now needed all the help it could get.

Pulling off my shirt, I slipped into the spelled flak jacket and strapped it on, tightening it so it couldn't be blown off me, then pulled my shirt back over it.

Next came the pump action spray gun—yet another of Milly's good ideas. Loading it with salt water from a sealed milk jug in the corner, I once more owed my friend. "Thank you Milly," I said under my breath.

With a shudder, the cellar door blew open. "Behind me, Alex!" I shouted.

I grabbed an arm's length sword off the wall and faced the open door with both weapons. Nothing moved. Even the sound of the wind seemed to have died down.

Gliding, as if it were on wheels instead of feet, a cloaked figure moved in front, blocking the light. Alex let out a whimper and scuttled backwards. I kind of wanted to do the same. The person's face was not covered by the cloak, but was instead distorted with some sort of spell, leaving the face a blur, like when you adjust the TV rabbit ears, and everything scatters across the screen. Flashes of eyes, mouth, and ears whipped around on the face, leaving me unable to give any sort of an impression of whether it was even a man or a woman.

Freaky.

"You will not come for the girl. She belongs to us." The voice was a monotone, giving nothing away.

I leaned forward on one of the swords. "Well, I can't do that. How do I know you aren't molesting her, or worse, making her into the next Martha Stewart?"

Silence. "You are insolent."

"I've been told that a time or two," I said, a distinct throb starting at the base of my neck. "Tell you what, I won't come for her if I can keep you tied up here in my basement and make use of you as I will. I mean, that's a fair trade—'"

The door slammed shut and I laughed. "Really? Locking me in my room because I've been naughty? That's the best you can do?"

I didn't hear the flames right away, not over my laughing. I shrugged, not worried in the least. There was a second way out leading to the trap door in my kitchen below the table. Trotting down the dirt hallway, I climbed the four-step ladder, grabbed the handle, and twisted hard to the left.

Alex whimpered and I frowned. Twisting it again, I jammed my shoulder against the trap door and pushed again. Nothing.

"Alex, help me," I said, feeling the first stirrings of panic. How had they known the trap door was even there?

The werewolf climbed the ladder beside me, his movements awkward and the space tight. "Now push, buddy."

Together we shoved hard on the door as the room filled with smoke. It wouldn't be the flames that killed us. Shit, shit, shit.

Even with both of us pushing with all we had, the door didn't budge; the wood didn't even splinter and break. They'd re-enforced it with a spell.

We were trapped.

15

He sped the whole way back from New Mexico to make up time, lights flashing on his SUV, sporting a massive hangover. O'Shea picked up Martins and filled him in before they raced to catch Adamson, the tracking device working well for once, showing him she'd gone home.

"There's got to be a ring of them working together. I think she's working with someone who kidnaps the kids, then she 'finds' them for a cost. A perfect sting on parents who are desperate." O'Shea actually wasn't sure of his new theory, he was just so pissed she'd dodged him again, he'd grasp at anything.

"Why wouldn't she just phone?"

"Taps."

"She doesn't look like the type to kill anyone, especially not her own sister. Nor the type to kidnap kids for money."

O'Shea snorted. "That's what she'd like us to believe, no doubt. But we can have a chat with her, try to loosen up her tongue." That brought a far too intimate image to mind, one that he quickly banished. He took the turn-off leading up to her home without pausing to even check the road sign. There were many nights he'd staked out her house early on, waiting, hoping for the break he'd need to finally put her behind bars. But what he'd seen was a woman who'd grown up with no family, alone in the middle of nowhere. He tried not to think about how it must feel for her to be alienated from everything she knew.

As they pulled into the yard, a strange sight met them. Four hooded figures stood near the back of the house, not trying to conceal themselves, but standing there, not moving. Smoke curled around their feet, looking like it came from the other side of the house.

"What the hell is this?" Martins asked.

O'Shea shrugged. "No idea."

They stepped out of the SUV in tandem.

Martins walked forward first, taking the lead, showing initiative, which was a surprise.

"Hello, we're looking for—" His words were cut off when the figures shot at them.

Except 'shot' wasn't quite the right word. They lifted their hands and *stuff* poured out of their fingertips, straight at the two agents. Bright blue and green, the 'stuff' zipped toward the junior agent first. Martins reacted faster than O'Shea thought he would, diving behind a hedge alongside the house. O'Shea used the SUV as a cover, his mind struggling to make sense of what he'd just seen.

"FBI Agents! Put your weapons down!" He fully expected them to react accordingly. Not so much, as it turned out.

They continued to send that sparkling crap toward both of the agents, which left the agents no other choice. Martins shot first, his aim way off the mark if the way the scarecrow in the field behind the figures jumped was any indication.

O'Shea leaned against the door and shot, his gun misfiring, not once or twice, but three times. "What the hell?"

Martins ran from the hedge across to a small pump house for better aim. Again though, his shots went wide—all four of them. This wasn't possible.

Smoke continued to curl out around the house, but that wasn't what stole his attention from the fire fight. It was the screaming.

O'Shea didn't think, he just burst from behind the Jeep, firing at the figures as he ran. A spiral of blue hit him, absorbing into his skin, and he held his breath, stumbling with the anticipation of pain, loss of vision, something bad. But there was nothing. Blinking, he stood back up and looked around. There was only one figure left and it stood five feet from him. He raised his gun as Martins ran up beside him.

The cloaked figure tipped its head sideways, as if considering them both.

"Lower your hands," O'Shea barked.

As if on cue the figure whipped its hands up, and O'Shea fired. He watched in horror as, in slow motion, the bullet curved almost ninety degrees to blow a hole in Martins' forehead right next to him.

O'Shea froze, unable to comprehend what had happened, his mind reeling at the impossibility of what his eyes were telling him.

More screaming. Adamson was screaming for him, his partner was dead and the bullet was from his gun.

His eyes flew back to where the figure had been, but it was gone along with the others.

In that moment, O'Shea felt his world spin out from under him; the only thing keeping him from losing it was the woman who cried out for his help. Holstering his gun, he pushed everything else away and ran toward her voice.

"Rylee. Scared," Alex whispered, his body pressed hard against mine as we crept forward. The only chance we were going to have was to break out through the flames and hope to hell we didn't catch fire. Not how I saw my day panning out when I got up that morning.

"I know, buddy. We're going to run fast, around the house to the Jeep," I said, scratching him behind the ear. "Understand?"

He huffed into the dirt. The smoke filled the room fast, my lungs ached, my eyes burning and my hope fading. If they, the bastards who'd taken India and attacked us here, had blocked the trapdoor, I doubted they would have left the cellar door to chance.

"Now," I said, prepping my body to hit hard, hoping I was wrong, hoping the door wouldn't be barred magically.

Our bodies hit in tandem and we were flung backwards, bitch-slapped by the power that held the door against us. I grabbed the jug of salt water and flung it on the door, but it did nothing; the spell was on the other side.

Intermittently howling and choking on the smoke, Alex sat on the floor, tears streaming down his face.

Even with all the weapons I had, there was nothing to break through magical barriers. There'd never been a need, and we were about to die because I hadn't been prepared.

I slumped to the floor, as a gunshot went off outside. "What the hell?"

Alex answered. "Guns." He paused. "Big guns. Man with gun here."

Man with . . .

"O'Shea!" I screamed. "Here, we're trapped!"

Another round of gunshots went off, then the sound of sirens. Shit, I'd never been so happy to have a constant tail from the agent that had tried to frame me for murder.

Coughing, I crouched back to the floor. Within moments, there was rattling on the cellar door and then it flung open. But it wasn't O'Shea.

"Milly!" I ran up the steps and caught her in a hug. She was crying, her hands white with powdered salt. The fire raged behind her, but it wasn't as close as I'd thought; the smoke had just been funneled toward us. Nice.

"I'm so sorry, Rylee."

"Hey, you made it in time, that's all that matters." Alex ran around us in circles, yipping until O'Shea ran into view. The wind, the real wind and not some magicked wind, picked up and blew the smoke and fire back out into the wheat field. That wasn't good either, but better than the alternative.

I turned to face him, putting Milly just behind me. I couldn't help it; we were a team, but when it came to O'Shea's anger, she didn't deserve to get the brunt of it.

But he didn't flare up. His face was pale, and it occurred to me he'd just seen magic for probably the first time in his life.

"Where's Mini-Me?" I asked, hoping to shake him out of his stupor.

He stared blankly at me.

I stepped closer and touched his arm, the chill of his skin evident even through the shirt. "Where's your partner?"

"Dead. I don't . . ." He shook his head. "How did this happen?"

I wasn't entirely sure what he was talking about. "Milly, what happened?"

"I knew you were in trouble, could feel the vibrations stronger than anything ever before." She pushed a long strand of dark brown hair off her forehead to reveal eyes that at times could be a soft green, and when she was pissed deepened to an almost neon green that flashed. Right now they were as soft and gentle as I'd seen them in a long time.

She went on. "I came out to the house, but they had already trapped you. O'Shea and his partner showed up—"

"Those people attacked us, we shot at them and . . ." O'Shea stared at me as if I was going to have the answers. Oh, this was not going to be good. "Our bullets *swerved*, came back and hit Martins, right in the forehead."

"Was it your bullet that swerved back?" My mind already caught on to the implications.

O'Shea frowned. "What does it matter? He's been killed in an impossible situation."

The sirens were almost here. "Listen, there isn't a lot of time. Think, O'Shea. You're going to tell people the bullets did whatever the fuck they wanted, swerved back and shot your partner with YOUR bullet? You're about to be implicated for murder."

His face paled. "They won't believe me." He put a hand to his head. "I wouldn't believe me."

I couldn't help it. "Just like you won't believe me when it comes to Berget."

Again, he just stared, his eyelids twitching as I watched emotions run across his face. Anger, fear, disbelief.

"Come on," I said. "We can't be here if you want to stay out of jail tonight."

"I'm not going with you. That'll only prove I'm guilty," he said. "When you run, it shows your guilt more than anything."

Well if that wasn't a dig at me, I didn't know what was. I laughed; I couldn't help it. Milly, standing beside me in her fashion-forward bright white pantsuit, was shaking her head.

"Rylee is right, Agent O'Shea. You can't prove your innocence. There aren't even any of the perpetrators here to point fingers at. Unless you did manage to shoot one of them?"

He shook his head. "No, but you're innocent until proven guilty. You should know that, Adamson."

Already the shock was wearing off and he was sliding back into this usually difficult self.

Shrugging, I turned my back. "Come on, Milly, if he wants to spend the rest of his life in jail for a murder he didn't commit, then let him."

We started to walk away, but it was Alex who stopped us with words he shouldn't have been able to utter. "Man with gun. He come with."

I spun in time to see O'Shea stumble backwards, eyes wide at really *seeing* Alex. He pulled his gun on the werewolf. I bolted toward them, but it wasn't me that got to O'Shea first. It was Milly.

She slammed him with a knock-out spell that rolled his eyes back into his head and dropped him to the ground.

"Good shot," I said.

"Thanks." She gave me a smile.

I grabbed Alex by the collar and the three of us ran around the side of the house as the fire trucks and police cars screamed into the yard. We pointed around the back of the house and they sped off in that direction.

As I shoved Alex into the Jeep, a black unmarked pulled in. "Damn."

Three hours later, we—Milly and I—were still explaining the same story over and over. I had been trapped in the cellar, Milly had showed up and heard gunshots, but neither of us had seen anything. Now it was up to O'Shea as to whether or not he dug his own grave.

We were released just as they brought O'Shea out of the house. In handcuffs.

I was surprised to feel a pang of guilt hit me. What the hell was that about? I tried to push it away, but it overrode any attempt I made to shrug it off. O'Shea hounded me for years; with him locked up, I wouldn't have to worry about who was following me around anymore. I let out a sigh. "You know this complicates things."

Milly touched my arm. "Your life would be easier without him in it."

"And yours would be easier without me in it," I said.

She ducked her head, shame flushing her face. "You're family, you and Giselle. The Coven gave me leave to help you on this case."

"Why?"

She didn't answer, our conversation interrupted.

O'Shea and his guards walked passed us. I wanted to make a smart remark; I knew that walk of shame. In fact, it had been O'Shea who'd walked beside me.

But I couldn't make the words form. He was as innocent as I was. Magic had a funny way of making humans believe the wrong thing.

We were allowed to stay while the police did their investigation; they told us ahead of time that it would likely take all night. They had lights on tall stands lighting up the yard as if it wasn't close to midnight in the middle of October.

Milly helped me make a late—very late—dinner of pasta and steamed veggies from the garden. Neither of us spoke as we cooked, except for the "pass the salt" variety of conversation. As soon as the food was ready, I put Alex's share in his bowl. He cleaned it in about thirty seconds flat—except for the carrots, which he left in the bottom of the dish.

"Eat your veggies, Alex," I said.

"No. Yucky, poopy," he grumbled, poking at them with the tip of one claw.

Milly leaned over. "You can have some dessert if you eat them."

Two bites later, and he was waiting patiently beside the fridge for ice cream.

I stood and scooped some of the tiger-striped dessert, the black and orange strips visible even through the thick plastic tub.

"I'll stay the night. But then I have to go," Milly said, finally breaking the silence.

"You won't get kicked out of your new club? Your new friends will let you come back?" I couldn't stop the words; maybe I didn't want to. She'd hurt me and I was not good at taking hurt, unless it was of the physical kind.

She glared at me. "And what would you do if your parents came back, if they said you could be a part of their family, but you'd have to give me and Giselle and Alex up? You'd do it."

A bitter laugh escaped my lips. "No, I wouldn't. They proved they don't give a shit about me. Why would I choose them over people who I love and care about, and who I thought felt the same?" I stood up, grabbed the plates from the table and stomped over to the sink. "One thing I do want to know, how long before you told your new friends I was looking for India?"

Her eyes filled with tears. "I never told anyone."

"Not even your new boy toy, whoever the hell that is?"

Her tears turned into a flush. Bingo. "What does it matter?"

I couldn't stop the anger bursting out. "Because someone left a nasty message for me only hours after I spoke with you, and because whoever has India knows I'm coming. And the only person I told about the case was you."

Milly stood, her white pantsuit splattered with flecks of spaghetti sauce. "He would not have shared it. I trust him."

"Just like you trusted the last one? And the one before that?"

Alex decided to chime in. "Before that?"

Milly's tears dried up. "You can be such a bitch, Rylee."

"At least I'm not a whore."

The world stilled around us. Never in all our time together had we let it go this far.

She spun and stomped upstairs, the guest bedroom door slamming behind her. I let out a sigh and slumped into my kitchen chair. I needed to apologize.

"Milly stay?" Alex asked, his tongue stained by the black coloring from the ice cream.

"No, I don't think so."

Slowly, I made my way up the stairs and tapped on the door to the guest room. "Milly, I'm sorry, I shouldn't have said that."

No answer.

Trotting back down the stairs, I made my way into the kitchen, glanced at the dirty dishes, and then decided to leave them.

My bed called to me and I still had to practice. Here at home I had a large punching bag, weights, medicine balls, and a climbing rope, all set up in my bedroom, what had previously been three bedrooms until I knocked the walls out. The rope was one of the things I hated most. When I'd bought the house, what was currently my bedroom was open through both floors, which meant I had a ceiling about twenty-five feet high.

I had two ropes hanging about five feet apart. I climbed the first one all the way to the top, reached across and slid down the second one. Then repeated the routine three times until my breath hitched in my chest. After that, came the punching bag, where I slid through my Muay Thai training. Then onto weights, then the medicine ball, and finally back to the ropes.

The final climb burned my hands, the rope fibers stinging, the cut in my forearm aching, sweat dripping into my eyes. But I couldn't stop, not until I'd done the whole routine.

Finally, I slid to the floor, body exhausted, heart tired, mind nearly numb enough for sleep.

Outside, the police still moved around. Every once in a while, I heard them over their walkie talkies, heard the rev of an engine start up.

Leaning back against my bedroom wall, I closed my eyes, letting the sweat dry on my skin. A cold nose pushed into my face and woke me up as the sun climbed the eastern horizon.

"Alex hungry."

I stood, stiff from the position I'd slept in, and headed to the bathroom. A quick shower and change of clothes left me feeling more optimistic. I'd apologize to Milly again, then things would be okay.

Within an hour of me waking up, the last of the forensics team, police included, had gone, leaving a smoldering wheat field, some yellow tape and a slew of tire tracks.

Milly came out to the back porch, a cup of coffee in her hand. Her eyes were cool, and wouldn't meet mine.

"Look, Milly, I'm sorry about last night. Really, I don't think of you that way." I meant the words. Sure she got around, but she always believed she was in love.

"I still think you can be a bitch," she said, but a smile was at the edge of her lips.

"Well, we both know that's the truth." I leaned back against the porch railing. "Are we okay then?"

She nodded. Neither of us spoke again until she'd finished her coffee. The obvious question had to be asked.

"Okay, Milly, time to confess. What's going on? You said you couldn't be around me, yet here you are." We sat on the back porch, staring out at the burnt field.

She took a deep breath, then laced her fingers together and placed them in her lap. She studied them carefully. "I'm to be your liaison. The people who took India are breakaways from the main Coven."

I flicked a piece of imaginary dirt off my jeans, giving myself a moment to think. "Why send you? I mean, no offense, but aren't you the baby of the group?"

High color flooded her cheeks. "Yes."

There was only one reason they would send a lesser-experienced witch after a group that broke away from the Coven.

"So are they trying to get rid of you by sending you after the rogues? Because that's what I see." And I didn't like it, not one bit. I might fight with her, but I would never deliberately try to hurt her; she was the closest thing besides Giselle that I had to family.

Milly's fingers tightened and she clenched her hands until the knuckles turned white, then slowly she relaxed. "They think I'm trouble. This would be a good way for them to use me up without just making an arbitrary decision to have me removed."

"How many rogues are we dealing with?" Together, we could take this group out, no problem.

"We aren't dealing with them. I am. I am to be your liaison while you rescue India, that's it. I will handle the black members," she said. We both knew Milly was good—very, very good—at what she did. She had to be to have survived this long without a Coven to back her up. But no matter how good she was, even she couldn't handle more than a few black witches at a time.

"Who'd you sleep with that you shouldn't have?" I leaned back against the porch pillar.

She stood, her eyes flashing, and stomped her way into the house, yelling over her shoulder through the open door. "Shut up! You don't know anything!"

"Do you love him at least?" I yelled back.

She paused in midstride, turning just her face back toward me, one hand on the kitchen table. "Yes."

"Is he worth it?"

"Yes."

I shrugged. "Well, then at least we know we won't both die in vain if it's for true love." I was betting it was anything but love. More like a serious case of the lusting hormones; that was Milly. She was a good friend, but I would hate to be one of the men who thought she loved them, and only them.

"Okay, so it was a fling," she said with a huff. "But seriously, how was I to know he was engaged to the Coven leader's daughter? He wasn't wearing a sign or anything."

I groaned. It couldn't get any worse.

Nope, wrong again. Alex trembled, and I turned to face where he was looking. There, galloping across the burnt field was the werewolf pack, teeth flashing as they howled their intent.

"They come to kill Alex. Stay till Alex is dead," he whispered.

16

"Time to go." I said, leaping to my feet and running through the house.

Milly trotted after us. "What's happening?"

"Pack, come. Kill," Alex said.

No more questions, we piled into the Jeep and spun out as the first of the pack hit the edge of the lawn. Snarling and howling, I knew they could scent not only Alex, but the blood from my stitches too. Not to mention the pool of blood from Martins's death.

Alex lay in the back of the Jeep, panting with fear. Milly stared out the window as the front-runner hit the side of the vehicle, almost tipping us over.

"Milly! Do something!" I yelled, battling with the steering wheel to keep up from going over. That would be bad on so many levels I didn't even want to consider.

"I can't. The pack has nothing to do with this case," she whispered, staring straight out front.

"And if they attack you?" I snapped, finally gaining some distance from the pack as we sped down the road, the tires squealing as they went from dirt to the tarmac of the paved road leading into town.

Milly started to cry. "I can't defend myself unless it's directly linked to the case or I'll be removed from the Coven and will be considered a rogue worthy of decapitation."

"Shit," I muttered. "That's just freaking fantastic. So you mean you're basically just a throwaway?"

She stiffened in her seat. "What did you call me?" We both knew she'd heard me; we'd been friends too long not to know exactly what was going down.

I took a left and headed toward Bismarck. We needed more than just a motel to keep the pack off our scent, and I needed a place I could get some info. I didn't have time to pamper Milly, much as she was my friend.

"You damn well know what a throwaway is. You're just going to get in the way, and cause more harm than good unless I'm using you for a shield. For them to put that restriction on you WAS a death sentence and you know it. Those bastards don't care about you, Milly!" I was shouting by the time I finished.

Alex was whispering in the back seat. "No fighting, no fighting."

"Stop this car right now. I am not a throwaway," Milly said, her voice as cold as a chunk of ice pressed against my skin.

"It's not a car, it's a Jeep." I glanced in the rear-view mirror. No werewolves galloping behind us. That was a plus.

"PULL THE FUCKING JEEP OVER!"

Well, that was a first. Both for the f-bomb, and the screaming. I didn't pull the Jeep over. "Milly, I don't think you're a throwaway, but that's how they're treating you."

I drove for another fifteen minutes on the main highway doing well over 60 mph, checking the mirror for a pack of werewolves galloping behind us before I pulled over, though it was still reluctantly. "If you still want to go, then go. You aren't a throwaway."

She got out, her hands shaking as she held the door open with both hands, almost as if she were holding herself up. "I know that. But they're everything I've fought so hard to have. And I need them. They have training techniques I can't learn anywhere else. I need to be a part of the Coven. They need to be my family now."

"And if they end up killing you? What then?"

"They won't let me die," she said, though her voice wavered. "Goodbye, Rylee."

She shut the door and started to walk down the shoulder, her thumb out. I waited until the first farm truck rumbled into view and she hopped in.

"I wouldn't be so sure of that, Milly." I couldn't deal with that loss right now. At the very least, she'd helped me to pinpoint the 'who' behind India's disappearance. A rogue Coven. That only made me feel slightly better about the case. It wasn't identical to Berget's, but still . . .

Checking my mirrors for cars and rampant werewolves, I pulled back onto the road when all was clear. As I drove, I wracked my brain for everything I knew about the Coven, or Covens in general.

"Okay, Alex. What do we know about witches?"

He grunted and slithered up to the front seat. "Milly."

"Yes, Milly is a witch." My heart ached more than a little. "Coven's have any number of people, but the core of them is always thirteen. Which means we're dealing with at least thirteen rogue witches. Yay."

Alex lifted his head and laughed. "Yay!" My sarcasm was lost on him completely.

On the open road, fields spilling out around us, I concentrated on what I had. I needed to find a deep mineshaft, needed to be prepared to face down the rogue Coven and, on top of that, avoid the pack that was probably setting up camp at my house, waiting for us to get back. And that's where all my gear was.

I stopped at the first hotel we came to, one I'd used a few times in the past. Running in, I booked a room in under three minutes. The fear that the pack would be on us if I left Alex by himself was strong, even though they didn't appear to be following us anymore, I wasn't taking any chances. Losing one friend in any given day was enough for me, particularly considering how few I had. Room key card in hand, I drove the Jeep into the underground parking, a large sheeted metal door closing behind us. Now the trick was going to be getting Alex into the room without being seen.

"Come on, we've got some flights to run up."

Alex gave a soft woof, his tail wagging as the flight from his rampaging pack mates was already forgotten.

Using the stairwell, keeping a hand on Alex's collar, we sprinted up the three flights with no problem. Peeking into the carpeted hotel hallway from the stairwell, I could see our room was at the far end. "Ready?"

He bobbed his head. "Yup."

I couldn't help but laugh, and for that alone, he was worth the pain in my ass he caused with all his pack issues. Sprinting again, we ran to our room, the key card in my hand and sliding through the lock before I'd come to a full stop, which meant we slammed through the door in a heap. Alex laughed and tried to start a wrestling match with me.

"Nope, not right now," I said, pushing him off me, the scratches on my arms a reminder of how lucky I was to be immune.

Flicking on the TV, I said, "You stay here, be quiet. I'll be right back." Alex ignored me as he leapt onto the king-sized bed and flopped down facing the TV.

Two trips later, I had brought up my overnight bag as well as a range of weapons from my Jeep. No way was I going anywhere else without them. For that matter, I was going to sleep in my flak jacket.

Next on the list was finding that mineshaft.

I dialed in Kyle's number from memory, hoping my little hacker was still up. A groggy hello answered the phone.

"Kyle, can you look up mineshafts for me around here?"

"Hello to you too, Rylee," he grumbled. A shuffling of papers and then I could hear him typing on the keyboard. "Lots of mineshafts, anything in particular?"

"Deep ones, two hundred feet or better," I said, switching the channels to a local news station.

"Only four that deep that I can find. Mines are deeper, but you just want the shaft?" His voice became clearer the longer we spoke.

"Yes. Send it here. I gotta go."

I gave him the hotel's fax number and hung up, not wanting to stay on longer than we had to and chance either a tap or a power failure due to my proximity. Plopping the phone back into its cradle, I stared at the TV. It was the main story that caught my eyes.

"FBI AGENT KILLS PARTNER IN COLD-BLOODED MURDER, THEN ESCAPES."

"You're in deep shit now, O'Shea," I said.

"Gun man in trouble?" Alex's voice picked up in intensity.

I stroked his head, soothing him. "Maybe."

The news reporter came on, her voice pitched all wrong for TV. The gist of it was that on transport, O'Shea (though they didn't name him) overpowered his guards and stole the unmarked car following the police cruiser he was in. The pictures looked like a bomb had gone off, like some high-end movie production chase scene had gone horribly wrong. Cars flipped over, debris everywhere, not to mention the people gawking at the edges of the scene as the helicopter flew overhead.

"Who do you think you are, O'Shea? Schwarzenegger?"

I turned the TV off. He was on his own now; I'd offered him help and he'd turned it down, stupid man.

Leaving Alex in the room, I took the elevator down to the lobby to see if Kyle had faxed me the info yet. The clerk, the same flustered young woman who'd

booked me in, went all wide-eyed when I said I had
a fax coming in.

"Oh, I'm sorry, we can't do that."

"Too late, I've already given him the number and if
you didn't want people sending in faxes it shouldn't
be on the welcome card." I flopped down said welcome pamphlet on the high counter that made me
feel like a little kid even in heeled boots.

Tight blond curls bounced as she shook her head.
"I'm so sorry, we can't . . ." a beeping noise interrupted her. Bless Kyle and his timing. My body ached,
my arm hurt, and all I wanted was to soak in a tub
and sleep for a few hours before seeking out the mineshaft. Sleeping against my bedroom wall hadn't been
the best of ideas. Damn, I needed Milly to keep me
on track.

The doors behind us slid open and a moment later,
a large hand pressed into the small of my back. "Did
you get us the room . . . honey?"

My eyes bugged out when I turned to stare at a more
than rumpled O'Shea standing at my side. "How did
you—"

"Oh, you know me, I can find you anywhere. Sweet-
heart." His voice was all smooth and silky, but his eyes
were wild. Not a good combo.

"Yes, and this lady here was just getting me my
paperwork." No need to make a scene in front of the
hotel staff.

O'Shea buried his face into my hair as the woman
lifted her eyes. "She can't see my face," he whispered
into my ear.

"Oh, I understand that . . . Poopsey."

He grunted as if I'd hit him. I snatched the papers out of her hand and threw a rumpled twenty over the desk. "That should cover any paper costs," I said over my shoulder. "Poopsey" snuggled into my hair as if we were long lost lovers.

The elevator slid open and we hustled inside. What I didn't expect was O'Shea almost pinning me up against the far wall, his face now against my neck.

"Cameras," he said, his lips tickling against my collarbone.

"You beyond owe me," I said. "I am going to own you after this." I was trying not to feel the hardness of his body against my own. I knew how the man worked out; like it was his religion. He wasn't the only one who knew how to tail a person. I placed my hands on his shoulders and tried very, very hard not to think about how this looked. When the door binged, O'Shea grabbed me around the waist and slung me over his shoulder.

Slapping me on the ass, he said, "If you're going to own me, I might as well make this worth it."

I squawked, but didn't protest overly much. His words were playful, but I could feel the strain in them, the tremor in his hands against me.

We got to the room and he slipped me off his shoulder, pressing himself against my back.

"Hey," I said, fumbling for the key card. "You might like all this touchy feely, ram-Rylee-against-the-wood-paneling business, but I can't get the damn door open if you don't give me some room."

O'Shea eased off me, just enough that I could take a deep breath and slide the key card through the reader.

With the click of the door, the air whooshed around us, a distinct scent of wet dog swirling towards us. Crap, this might be a problem.

"Ryleeeeee!" Alex howled out, his black fur soaking wet, the sound of the shower still running. Bugger, I hadn't thought to tell him to stay out of the water.

The door slammed and I spun, pinning O'Shea against it, tipping a short sword up into his groin. "Don't pull your gun, big man."

He stared over my shoulder, his eyes wide. "What the hell is that?"

"Did you hear me?" I didn't ease up on the blade.

"Adamson." Mild tremors went through him. Moving slowly, he lifted his hands up over his head. "Now, what the hell is that? It can talk?"

I stepped back, bumping into Alex who peered around my legs. "This is Alex. He's a werewolf."

Alex, being who he was, lifted one giant paw and flopped it at O'Shea in a loose wave.

"A werewolf?" He started to lower his hands and I poked him with my knife.

"No guns."

"Does he bite?"

Alex shook his head. "No bites."

O'Shea pushed himself back against the door, his eyes wide and so dilated I would have thought he was high if I didn't know better. "A talking werewolf. . . before, I thought maybe I had been hearing things." His voice was soft and his eyes lifted to mine. I'd only ever seen his nearly-black eyes angry, not this shell-shocked confusion. It actually made me feel bad for him.

I lowered the sword, propping it against the wall next to the bathroom. Just in case. "Alex is not like most werewolves. He's submissive, and for all intents and purposes, I'm the boss. Right?" I dropped a hand on Alex's damp head. He pushed into my fingers, forcing me to scratch behind his ears.

"Go dry off, Alex." I pointed to the bathroom. With a grunt and a wag of his tail, he did as I said, leaving O'Shea and me alone.

"First of all, how did you find me?" I slipped out of my jacket.

O'Shea's eyes narrowed. "I thought you didn't carry guns."

I fingered the shoulder holster I wore, then turned so he could see the back, how it crisscrossed and held the sheaths for my blades. "Swords, not guns."

"Why?"

Big breath in. *Realize he has no idea about your world.* "As you may have noticed, guns and bullets do weird things when placed up against the supernatural. Like take corners and kill people they shouldn't. Swords don't. And if they are edged and spelled right . . ." His eyes continued to widen and I thought about what I'd said, and how he'd not answered my first question.

"I'll explain everything, if you tell me how you found me. Otherwise, I'll pick up that phone over there and dial 9-1-1," I said, doing my best not to be too bitchy.

"I've been profiling you for years. You have a pattern. Every fourth time you need a room, it's either this hotel or the one across the street when you are on a . . . case." He leaned forward, placing his elbows on his knees.

Hmm. That was interesting and not in a good way. If he could find me that easy, we were going to have to move, sooner rather than later.

Hands clenched into his dark slacks. "This can't be happening."

I barked out a laugh and kicked off my boots. "Really? This is my life, man. And it looks like you're about to get a serious dose of the true reality of this world. Want to tell me what really happened when I was locked up in the cellar with the ones who you were shooting at?" I was betting there was more to the story than he'd told me already.

"Besides my partner being shot with my gun even though I wasn't pointing it at him?" His dry tone told me he was coming out of the funk.

"Yes." Best to keep things short and sweet at this point.

"They hit me with—" O'Shea flipped his hands in the air and then jumped as the blow dryer came on in the bathroom. "How can he manage that with those claws?"

"It's one of the things that takes him a while, but he can manage," I said, going right back to my original question. "What did they nail you with?"

Pushing off the door, he started to pace the small space between the far window and the door. "It was, I don't know, a spell?" He lifted his eyes to mine for confirmation, and it hit me how fast our relationship had changed. All of a sudden he was looking to me for help.

"Most likely. Can you tell me what it looked like? Colors, density, sound?" I leaned back on the bed, letting out a sigh. This hotel had good mattresses. I flipped an arm over my eyes. "All those things can help me figure out what they might have spelled you with."

The bed squeaked and I looked out from under my arm to see O'Shea crawling toward me, his eyes dilated, a smile on the edge of his mouth as he took in a deep breath. Oh crap. "Never mind," I said, rolling away from him. "I know what they hit you with."

"You do? How?" Those dark eyes roved my body as if I were naked. Yup, though that was not the worst spell he could have been hit with, and at least I knew how to counter it.

I was already slipping on my jacket. "I'm going to go and get something to break it. You stay here." Already my boots were back on.

O'Shea stood and his eyes clouded over. "You aren't going to tell me what it is?" Now that was a defiant thread of anger I heard.

"It'll only freak you out." I took a breath. "Alex, stay in the bathroom until I get back."

He barked out. "Yuppy doody."

A dark eyebrow lifted in my direction. I shrugged. "He's got a weird lingo. You'll get used to it."

The former FBI agent snorted. "This is not a permanent arrangement."

It was my turn to snort. "Really? And who else is going to believe that your bullet went fucking about on its own trajectory to kill your partner? Who else is going to believe that you have a spell on you that has messed with your emotions, ability to think clearly, not to mention your ability to control yourself?"

He blanched and sat down on the edge of his bed.

I shook my head. "I won't be long. Don't move and don't kill Alex, because that would seriously piss me off, and right now I am your only friend in this whole messed up world."

Slamming the door behind me, I trotted to the stairs. Damn, this was getting complicated.

17

With Adamson gone, O'Shea finally let himself relax, or at least take a breath. His mind was full of things he should not be thinking about. The feel of her skin, the flush in her cheeks, the curve of her ass under his hand. What was wrong with him? Ever since the . . . incident at the farmhouse, he couldn't get her out of his head, couldn't stop the thoughts of her naked and writhing below him—maybe didn't want to. He'd been crawling across the bed toward her. Was this what that blue and green stuff they'd shot at him was doing? That spell? He scoffed at the idea and then his thoughts swung back to Adamson.

In an attempt to take his mind, and better yet the mind between his legs, off her and to gain back some control, he flicked on the TV. And there he was in full living color, a wanted man, armed and dangerous, charged with gunning down his own partner and possibly kidnapping one Rylee Adamson.

"Ah crap," he muttered, turning the TV up slightly, the clear voice of the female news anchor making his ears buzz. All he could see was that as beautiful as she was, there was no comparison to his girl.

Everything around him froze. His girl?

Sweat beaded on his forehead as he tried desperately to make sense of what was happening to him. Bullets swerving, magic spells, and werewolves? It sounded like a bad joke at a geek convention.

He lay back on the bed and closed his eyes. Adamson thought she had a cure for what ailed him. A part of him hoped she did. The other very vocal part wanted nothing to do with any sort of a cure. For the first time in his life, passion overruled his better senses and, though logically he knew it, surprisingly it wasn't bothering him as much as it should have.

Eyes closed, he could see her clear as day, smiling up at him; he tasted her lips under his, watched those amazing eyes light up just for him.

"I am in so much trouble," he said softly.

From the bathroom came an unexpected reply from Alex. "You's in trouble."

Yes, when even a werewolf could see you were sinking fast, it had to be bad.

Lugging three grocery bags back up to the room, I stumbled when the door opened for me.

O'Shea had his shirt un-buttoned and his hair was a mess. "Alex heard you coming."

The werewolf had not listened to me and was even now sitting on the window seat staring out at the traffic below.

"Alex, stay away from the window."

He slumped and slid to the floor in a comical move that left him half sitting, half resting against the chair. I bit back the smile as I took in his chagrined face.

I wasn't surprised Alex alerted O'Shea.

"Come on, Agent. Let's get you into the bath." I held up the plastic bags and jiggled them. "Then we've got to get out of here. If you can find me that easy, the pack won't be far behind if they're tracking us, and close behind the pack may be those little lovelies who locked me in the cellar and killed your partner."

I started the bath, the scent of wet dog lingering even with the bathroom fan on. Running the water on full hot, I poured six large containers of salt into the tiny tub. Looking over my shoulder, I considered the options. There weren't any others. If we were going to break the spell on O'Shea, he was going to have to cram his overlarge frame into the standard-sized hotel bath. Tight fit was an understatement; it would be like jamming a werewolf into a Chihuahua's winter sweater.

"Come on, in you go." I gestured to the tub.

A smile quirked across O'Shea's lips. Very slowly, he started to peel out of his clothes.

"Clothes on big man," I said. "The spell hit those too, and since we don't have spare clothes in your size, everything's getting dunked. The only thing we have to be grateful for is that it seems to have some sort of delay on it; otherwise, the spell would've had you in its grip far sooner."

His smile slipped, and I wondered at the thoughts whipping through that head of his without his usual control to keep things in line. I had a feeling he was going to be a mighty grouchy man when the spell was taken off him and he remembered how he'd been acting toward me.

I laughed out loud at the thought. "I mean it, all of you in there." I pointed at the tub, which seemed to be shrinking by the moment with O'Shea standing there beside it.

With some difficulty, he squished into the nearly scalding water, a long hiss erupting out of him.

"Too hot?" I kept my face a mask of innocence.

"No, I like it." Again his eyes roved over me. Buggers, maybe he really did have a thing for me. Nope, best not to go down that route; too dangerous by far.

"You need to soak for at least ten minutes, make sure you dunk your head. We'll put your shoes in after." I stepped out into the main room.

While I waited for O'Shea, I started to go through the list of mineshafts Kyle sent me. There were four, as Kyle said, and one was cemented, so that was a no go. Which left only three to consider. One of those three fell short of the two hundred feet by six inches. But if there was one thing I'd learned, it was if a Shaman said two hundred feet or better, they meant it in a very literal sense.

I stared at the last two mineshafts, my gut clenching as the details became clear. One was relatively new, only fifty or so years old, and there were ongoing happenings around it, including a still active mine with employees working there on shift 24/7.

The other was pretty much out in the middle of nowhere; the closest town and actual road was over sixty miles away from it. Not to mention—I flipped the page to make sure I was getting the facts right—it was closer to two hundred and fifty feet and was about to be capped as several people had fallen into it over the last few years. Kyle sent me a newspaper clipping on the last victim of the mineshaft fall. "The body was so badly mangled that the coroner repeatedly questioned the rescuers on the location of the body. He stated that it looked like some of the wounds had not been inflicted by the fall itself, but by some other source."

Interesting they didn't actually mention what the other source of wounds might be.

Alex let out a fart and rolled over, his tongue lolling out in a toothy grin.

I opened the window with a grimace and, as I turned back to the bed, a soggy, grumpy agent stormed out of the bathroom.

"My clothes are ruined," he snarled.

"Ooh, now that was the O'Shea I'd been missing," I said, shrugged, and continued. "Better that than having you strip tease for me and putting the clothes in after."

His face slowly turned red and the veins running up the side of his neck pulsed, but he said nothing.

I smirked and enjoyed the momentary silence. It didn't last long.

"You said you'd explain everything," he said, his eyes hard and flinty. He was not a happy agent.

Alex jumped up and looked out the window as I started to give O'Shea the rundown. Witches, daywalkers, werewolves, and ogres. Just to start. He dried his hair with a towel, which gave it a very, very sexy rumpled look.

Sexy? Who said that? I caught the turn of my thoughts before they could get me into trouble. Damn, but it was sexy. His hair was still damp, and the moisture caught the little bit of light coming through the window. He leaned back and ran one hand through his hair, his bicep flexing under the wet cloth of his shirt. I scrambled back, blinking. Maybe I'd got some of the spell on me? Like when he'd me pinned up against the wall in the elevator, or thrown me over his shoulder. I was only *mostly* immune to magic. Some of it could stick. Damn, this was not the time to have my immunity fail me.

Problem was, being a supernatural myself, when I *did* get some sort of spell on me, I was way more susceptible to it than others. Almost like an allergy. What made O'Shea horny was about to send me over the deep end of whoredom. I was about to make Milly look like the Virgin Mary. Crap. I tried to sidle past him to the bathroom, but all I could think about was how I'd kissed him the other day, the sharp tang of mint on his tongue, how his body felt holding me against the wall.

"This is bad," I whispered, my hand reaching for his hair as I struggled to make it to the bathroom without pouncing on him.

"What's your issue now?" He grumped at me, the deep bass of his voice giving me chills in a not unpleasant way, his dark eyes glaring at me. Never in all the years he'd tried to pin Berget's death on me had I thought him attractive. Of course, I'd hated him with a passion, and it would have been impossible for me to see past that.

I clenched my jaw, pulled my fingers back, and ran the last few steps into the bathroom, slamming the door behind me. My body shook with the need to feel him against me, skin on skin. I let out a low groan and sat on the edge of the tub, relishing the unfamiliar sensations rippling through me. A sex life was just not something I'd engaged in. Too dangerous to get close to people, not to mention messy as hell. But this, as much as it was a spell, was in its own way, safe.

Striping down, I could imagine his hands roving my body as he undressed me, kissing his way down to my navel, and then dipping lower. Again, I let out a groan; let my fingers caress the skin of my belly and imagined it was his lips.

"Adamson," the door creaked open. "Are you hurt?"

"Oh, fuck me," I whispered, meaning it whole-heartedly. I was half-naked and he was coming in, his body filling up the space in the tiny bathroom. I gripped the edge of the tub, my shirt on the floor, bra undone and pants unzipped. His breath caught; I heard it a split second before I lifted my eyes to his.

Tension filled the small room and he shut the door behind him. "Put your clothes on." There was a definite crack in that voice.

I stood and stepped toward him. "What are you going to do if I don't? Handcuff me?"

I looked up at him now, brazen with the spell working fast and hard on me, wishing he'd do the same. Even knowing it was a spell, my brain screaming at me that I didn't even like O'Shea, never mind want to bed him, I couldn't seem to stop.

Running one finger up the damp shirt clinging to his ribs, I said, "Is that what you're going to do? Handcuff me?"

"The same spell has you, doesn't it?"

I shrugged and smiled up at him, running my tongue over my lips. "Maybe."

He swallowed hard. "Into the tub."

"Only if you come with me." I leaned forward. Just a little closer and I could almost taste that minty flavor of his mouth. A shiver rippled the length of my body as the heat between us spiked, my skin prickling with anticipation. "Touch me, please." I wanted his hands on me so badly I didn't care if I begged.

Putting his hands on my shoulders, he started to set me back toward the bath, his mouth a tight line. A smile curved my lips into what I knew was a sultry twist, one I'd seen Milly turn many a man's head with.

Feeling bold, I slid my hand across his chest, my fingers finding their way in past the buttons. Smooth, hard abs trembled under my fingertips, and I couldn't stop the sigh that escaped me. "Please."

His hands slid down my shoulders to my elbows where he tightened his grip, pinning my arms to my sides. "In a minute."

With one smooth motion he picked me up and dropped me into the tub, the water exploding out all around me. Sputtering and gasping, I sat up, the spell receding quickly with the salt water. O'Shea stared down at me.

"Better?"

I took quick stock. My brain functioned fine, and while I still ached with some serious hormones, I knew it wouldn't have mattered who it'd been, I would have thrown myself at them.

"Nothing personal," I said, slicking my hair back. "Damn, that was a potent one for it to stick to you and then still have enough juice left to hit me."

O'Shea nodded. "Does that sort of thing happen often?"

"No." I dunked down under the water, held my body under for ten seconds, and resurfaced, letting my body float in the salt water. My bra and jeans would survive the dunking, but I'd have to wipe down my all leather jacket with salt water and condition it right away. Shit, what a pain in the ass. But it wasn't as bad as it could have been.

If only O'Shea knew what we'd just avoided.

As if reading my mind, he asked the one question I'd hoped he wouldn't.

"What would have happened if you hadn't known how to break that . . . spell?" He leaned against the bathroom counter, cool as could be. Like nothing had happened. Good, if he could ignore the blood-pounding moments, so could I.

I stood, and he handed me a towel. Stripping off my bra behind the towel, I wrapped my body with the fluffy white material. "We would be going at it hot and heavy right now."

He nodded. "I got that much. But who really cares who you knock boots with?"

Blinking, I realized this was going to be a steep learning curve for the agent—strike that, former agent. I shimmied out of my wet jeans and left them in the water. "How easy would we have been to find if we couldn't stay out of each other's pants? And if no one was looking for us, we'd have just banged the life out of each other. Literally."

It was only a slight shift of his body, but I saw him recoil as the implications set in; in fact, I saw the very moment he got it. His eyes widened and his jaw actually dropped. "You mean we would have fucked each other to death?"

"Yup. Eventually. I suppose it wouldn't be a bad way to go, and it certainly would be hard to pin on anyone." I held my hand out. "Another towel, please."

He handed me a smaller towel, which I wrapped my hair in. "As soon as we dry out, we've got to move. The Coven who has India are the ones who attacked you and tried to kill me, and they will no doubt make another attempt to stop me."

"Why's that?"

"Because I have a reputation for being stubborn," I said. "And they know it."

He snorted.

I glared at him.

Putting his hands back on his hips he nodded, the hint of a smile flicking across his lips. "It doesn't take supernatural ability to know that."

18

In less than an hour we were on the road. I wanted
to check out the mineshaft while there was still day-
light and we were less likely to run into any uglies.

"Uglies?" Alex barked from the back seat.

O'Shea cringed. It would take him some time to get
used to the werewolf.

"Yup, uglies. What are they, Alex?" I wanted him
to keep talking. Things had gotten awkward as we'd
piled into the Jeep, my hand brushing against O'Shea's
thigh by accident, the heat flaring between us.

"Demons." Alex whispered and crouched low in
the seat, his tail no longer wagging.

"You have got to be kidding me."

I glanced over at O'Shea. "No. YOU have got to
stop saying that. This is reality." I debated whether
or not to mention the Arcane Division of the FBI.
They might welcome him with open arms, but then,
as I glanced over at him, they might not. Most likely,
nobody was supposed to know about it. Certainly not
me and definitely not someone who was on the lam
for killing his partner.

"If I can prove this exists, this supernatural side of
things, they might re-instate me," he said.

We pulled off the main road onto a barely discernible track that had at one point been the main drag into the mine. Now it was filled with potholes and washouts. Just one more reason I had a serious love for my Jeep. I threw it into four-wheel drive and hit the gas, ignoring O'Shea's statement.

"Bumps!" Alex screeched from the back as we started to bounce down the track. I didn't take it easy, despite O'Shea's grunts of displeasure as he was jostled in the passenger seat. This was something Alex loved and I wouldn't deny him this small pleasure, not with each day being one closer to the day the pack might finally catch him.

"Slow the hell down, Adamson." O'Shea snapped after his head got thrust into the not-so-well-padded roof.

"Almost there, I think." I took a deliberate sharp turn in order to hit one last big rut in the road. Alex squealed and I couldn't help laughing. "Enjoy the ride, Agent. You never know when it might be your last."

He glared over at me, but said nothing, his hand gripping the Holy Shit handle with decidedly white knuckles. "Fuck." He muttered it just low enough that I had to strain to hear him.

I couldn't resist poking at him. "What was that?"

"FUCK!" Alex screeched from the back of the Jeep, and I burst out laughing. A glance at O'Shea and I caught a smile twisting his lips.

"Admit it, that was funny." I gunned the Jeep and slammed on the brakes so we skidded through the loose scree. I mean, who had a werewolf yell out "fuck" in the back of their Jeep?

"No."

Of course, that only made me laugh harder. Never had I been so distracted on a case before, but in a weird way it felt like a good fit.

I turned the Jeep off. "Here we are."

Lucky enough, I'd been right and there were no "uglies," so to speak. But then, the gateway through the Veil wasn't open either. The mineshaft wasn't particularly narrow, about two and a half people wide. Walking around the edge of it, I let my fingers trail over the metal rim, feeling the jagged cuts where grappling hooks would have been jammed in, in order to repel down. In my mind I tried to imagine how it would look.

"There's just enough for two people and a kid," O'Shea said, coming to the same conclusion I had.

Damn, how many others had this Coven stolen? "Have there been a lot of other missing kids lately? You know, ones with no leads?"

O'Shea gave a sharp nod. "Three. All in the last six months. All within a two-day drive of here."

Double damn, that was not good.

Leaning over the rim, I put my weight in my heels as I stared into the pitch black hole. How terrifying would it be as a little kid, to be forced to go there with people in cloaks, people you didn't know or trust?

I took a deep breath, the faintest scent of sage wafting up to my nose, a common herb burned in all Covens. "Alex, come smell."

Loping over to me, he stuck his head down the pipe. I laid a hand on his collar, just in case.

"Witches," he grunted, then took another sniff. "Demons." He whimpered, and on the third sniff, he cocked his head. "One more." He took a long drag and curled his lip, showing his teeth. "Don't know. Funny smell."

Hmm. It was never good when Alex couldn't identify a scent. "Okay, let's go get ready."

"That's it?" O'Shea asked, peeking into the pipe. "We don't dive in?"

"Not without the right gear—of which you have none. Mine is all back at my house, where the pack is currently staked out. Which means we need to go where I can get us the right weapons. Unless you have a grappling hook, harness, and rope stowed away in your pants pocket?"

He didn't answer except with a glower.

I cast out for India while O'Shea mulled that over. She was not any easier to trace here, but I could feel her. The fear was almost gone, but the most important thing was that she was alive. They—the Coven— hadn't used her for a sacrifice yet.

O'Shea followed me and Alex back to the Jeep. "You didn't kill her, did you?"

I froze between one step and the next, but didn't turn around to face him. In a way, I was surprised it had taken him this long. "You finally believe me?"

The shuffle of clothes told me he'd shrugged. "I'm having a hard time with believing any of this, but I'm seeing it whether I want to or not."

"Maybe one day I'll tell you the whole story," I said, knowing that would pique his interest.

He caught up to me in split second, grabbed my arm, and spun me to face him. "You didn't tell us the truth?"

In all the interrogations after Berget had gone missing, I'd adamantly stuck to my story. We'd been at a park, she'd been on the swings one second, gone the next. Nothing else to say. But how was I going to explain to the police what had really happened? It was bad enough they thought I was guilty, that I thought I was guilty, even though I'd done nothing. All along, that was the problem. I hadn't saved her and that made me guilty in my own eyes. In our parent's eyes.

"You'd believe me now, because you've seen what the world holds in truth. But not then," I said, brushing his hand off my arm.

We started to pile into the Jeep when a hair-raising screech spun me around, my eyes searching the skies above for the only thing that could have made the sound.

Harpies; three of them. They were each the size of a large cow, well over a thousand pounds per, and had greasy brown feathers covering their lumpy, bird-like bodies. While legends sometimes pinned them as having the upper bodies of beautiful women, that wasn't quite true. Hypnotizing eyes making you believe they were beautiful were the main gear the Harpies employed when it came to seduction. They didn't look like much as far as being dangerous, but the two sets of claws—one off the bottom of their feet and one set at the tips of their wings—were enough to cut a man in half with a single squeeze. They could rip my Jeep open like a tin can and have us for dinner without breaking a sweat.

Damn it all to motherfucking hell, this was about to get ugly. The last time I'd faced Harpies had been five years ago, and that had only been one Harpy. It'd taken Giselle and Milly at my side to knock her out, and we'd barely made it out alive.

I pulled a sword out as the first Harpy struck, her claws skimming precariously close to my stomach, ripping through my thin t-shirt and exposing the flak jacket below. Spinning, I swung my blade overhead, arcing toward where the Harpy's wings should be. My aim was true and the spelled sword cut deep into what would be the bicep of the Harpy, taking her right wing completely off. Howling and flailing, she rolled on the ground, brilliant red blood spurting in a fountain from where her wing had been only moments before. She flopped on the ground, arterial spurts shooting out around us.

That had been lucky, like as in ridiculously so. Of course, there were two more, so I wasn't counting us out of danger just yet.

"Get in!" I ran for the Jeep.

O'Shea listened for once, and the doors slammed shut as I peeled out.

"No smell Harpies." Alex whimpered. Of course he hadn't smelled them before; no doubt, they'd watched us from a distance, flying in high enough.

"It's okay," I said, though it wasn't. "O'Shea, you're going to have to take the wheel, or take one of my swords and try to fend them off. They're territorial, so you just have to buy us time."

"You drive, I'll fight."

"Don't look them in the eyes, no matter what."

O'Shea took my offered—and bloodied—sword and rolled down the window.

"Why?"

We hit a bump and I fought with the steering wheel, no longer enjoying the pot-hole filled road. "Think a version of the spell that was on you and me, except you'd get to 'knock boots' with *them*, and then they'd eat you."

Without a word, he slipped off his seatbelt and slid halfway out the window, his butt hanging on the edge. A part of me was starting to admire the former agent. He was not only doing as he was told, but he did it without arguing. Damn, I really didn't want to like him.

A screech from above us that might as well have been inside the cab lifted the hair all over my body. Alex howled, adding to the noise, but it didn't affect my concentration. Ahead was a Y in the road. To the right waited the main highway and possible safety. To the left waited more of the badlands. Decisions, decisions.

O'Shea hollered and his body flexed as he swung. I didn't have to see to know what was happening. I could almost feel the missed thrust of the sword.

"Get back in!" I hoped O'Shea could hear me. One of his hands slipped back in and gripped the Holy Shit handle, and he yanked his body back in, the sword dented.

"We're going to pit species against species," I said, gunning the Jeep and cranking the wheel hard to the left. The four-wheel drive was a godsend as we blasted across the open badlands with nowhere to hide from the two remaining Harpies.

O'Shea clicked on his seatbelt. "What do you mean species against species?" He had to yell to be heard over Alex and the Harpies.

I gripped the wheel and kept my foot on the gas. "Just wait. You'll see." A part of me wondered at my reasoning. Maybe I didn't want O'Shea to think all the monsters were nasty. Some of them were downright stunning in their beauty.

"I'll give you a hint," I said. "Ever read anything by Peter S. Beagle?"

We hit a bump and then something, presumably a Harpy, hit the Jeep and we teetered on two wheels. There was the screech of metal meeting and giving to talons as the Harpy dug into the hard top.

"This side!" I motioned with my head for the two boys to throw their weight to my side of the Jeep. Alex obeyed, as did O'Shea. His body jammed against mine. Our eyes met for a split second, and I thought I saw something there in those dark depths. This was bad, we could die, yet I'm sure I saw fire flare inside him as if he were . . . enjoying this.

Then the moment was over; all four wheels hit the ground and we careened down a slope, the Jeep skidding sideways as Alex whimpered in the back.

Wind whistled through the new tears in the metal roof; flashes of dark brown between the bursts of sunlight were all I could see of the Harpies, but it was enough. At the bottom of the slope, the ground leveled out into flat hard surface, perfect for the Jeep to pick up speed. In a few short moments, we were doing over sixty.

"They're well behind us," O'Shea said, half turned in his seat, and I glanced at him, his eyes still glittering. He *was* enjoying this.

I didn't let up on the throttle, though; I knew what was coming. Ahead of us was a large rock that stuck out of the ground like a mini mountain. Spinning the wheel, I tucked the Jeep in beside it, facing the Harpies. They hovered for another split second, and then they exploded toward us with a flurry of wings.

"Oh shit," O'Shea said.

I lifted a hand and turned the Jeep off. "Just wait."

"Are you crazy?"

I rolled down my window and prayed I was right. The distant thunder of hooves answered my pleas. This was the territory of the Tamoskin Tribe—or more accurately, herd.

I felt more than saw O'Shea go still beside me.

"Tell me I'm seeing things."

From off the plains thundered the Tamoskin Herd, their coats a myriad of colors, shining and glossy in the sun. From Paints, to blacks, chestnut, and white, and a little of everything in between, there was only one thing they all had in common besides their equine bodies.

The gleaming golden horn jutting from the middle of their foreheads.

19

"**Y**up," I said. "You're seeing things all right."

The herd of unicorns split into formations, four to be exact, surrounding the Harpies, who wailed and screeched, obviously pissed off at being tricked into crossing over the boundary line. I knew though they wouldn't back down. A Harpy rarely backed away from a fight, especially when it came to their mortal enemies.

It was a bit like watching a show, the kind you go to the local fair to see, where riders take their horses through complex patterns, barely missing each other as they gallop past one another. This was in some ways no different, only it was unicorns and no riders. The Tamoskin herd swirled and dove, moving like water, smooth and effortless as they engaged the Harpies.

I glanced over at O'Shea, who sat transfixed by the sight. Even I was hard pressed to tear my gaze away from the awesome scene in front of us. It wasn't every day you saw a childhood story come to life in front of you, that you saw legends held power in them still.

"Never in my life . . ." His voice awed to a bare whisper.

Alex leaned forward and put his head on my shoulder. "Beautiful."

It was that; even though the sight was a deadly game the two species played, it was no doubt one of the most amazing, beautiful things I'd ever seen. A tightening started in my chest, a pang I'd pushed away for so long. It wasn't for O'Shea I'd done this.

It was for me.

The dark side of the supernatural saturated me, was all I saw anymore. Most days I didn't pause, I just assumed everything around me was dark and ugly. Like losing Milly, like Giselle losing her mind, like me losing Berget.

But this was the bright side, literally, of the supernatural. I found myself standing outside of my Jeep, the pang in my chest thrumming as I walked toward the battle. One of the Harpies was down, her body pin-cushioned by horns, her chest rising in shallow breaths.

A hand grabbed me from behind. "Get in the Jeep," O'Shea said, biting off each word with a tug on me.

I looked at him, giving him the full force of my eyes, knowing the three colors would shift and swirl with the emotions rising in me. "No."

There was no way I could explain what it was I needed, or why in this moment I chose to find something bright to cling to, only that I had to. Something about this case, something about dealing with O'Shea was, in a sense, forcing my hand. If I was being honest with myself, it was the guilt this case brought up, the ugliness from my past. I needed to know there was more than the blasted ugliness in this world where I lived.

A need for the bright, for the brilliant and pure side of the supernatural, called to me, and I heeded that cry.

My feet carried me to the edge of the battle, where the remaining Harpy screeched well above the unicorns, her voice echoing out across the badlands.

"Tracker, you will die for this. I will gorge on your heart." The words weren't all that unexpected, and it wasn't the first time I'd been threatened.

I nodded. "I hear you." Even as she threatened me, I could show the respect due. I was a mere Tracker, a human that had somewhere in her family history gained some funky abilities. But Harpies were legendary, creatures that had been around far longer than humans.

She peeled away from the herd, swirling back into her own territory. It was going to be difficult to get past her. No doubt, she would sit on the mineshaft waiting for us to come back.

The herd, or Crush as they were known, if you want to get specific, turned their attention on me. Eyes of all colors, from pale grey to black, the traditional violet to bright blue and green eyed me with open curiosity.

But it was the lead Stallion who stepped out of the Crush toward me, jet-black body gleaming in the sun, sparkling with iridescent rainbows across the black satin of his coat.

Child, you are broken.

His words sliced through my mind, as if his horn had pierced me clean through. O'Shea gasped, and I had no doubt he'd heard the same words.

Tears slipped from my eyes. "Yes." I lowered my face.

The tip of his golden horn lifted my chin up, my eyes meeting his. A wave of warmth washed over me, empathy, pity, and faith flowed from him to me. He manipulated my ability to sense others, but I didn't care.

You have a far way to journey yet, do not lose heart. A bright spot in the darkness; that is what you can be, if you choose. Steel your resolve. You are not alone. There are those who cheer you on, those you cannot possibly know; those who believe you will be the one to break his hold on us. Do not let your guilt blind you to the future that awaits you.

Blinking, I wiped the tears from my face. "Whose hold? What are you talking about?"

If unicorns could smile, this one did. *I have said too much already.*

At some unspoken signal, the Crush of Unicorns spun in unison swirling around us, close enough to smell the lavender and whisper of jasmine clinging to their hides. Their split hooves pounded out a rhythm around us, rattling my bones until my heart beat in time with theirs.

Just like that, they were gone. There was no malice in them, not even toward us, who'd brought their age-old nemesis right into their territory.

The dust swirled and settled, the sun beat down, and it was like nothing had happened. Minutes passed; the silence thick and heavy. It was O'Shea who finally broke the spell the Crush cast.

He stepped in front of me. "Question her. She's our only chance for info on the Coven."

Though I didn't need him to tell me what I already knew, he was right. Turning, I headed over to the

Harpy the unicorns had pinioned. She was barely breathing, blood pouring from multiple punctures.

"Well played, Tracker, well played," she coughed out, her mouth twitching.

"Why are you working for a rogue Coven?" The sound of my voice seemed so harsh and unreal after hearing the Stallion's voice inside my head, feeling his emotions in my heart.

The Harpy shuddered. "They are powerful; they spelled us so we had no choice. Please, free my sister. She is young yet, a child in our years."

Ah, fuck.

I crouched down to her. "You know I can't. I'm seeking another child, one the Coven stole."

"You swore an oath once, Tracker. To seek out and save any child you could, for anyone who would ask for your help. Do you renounce this oath now?" Her eyes, though dulling as death stalked her body, filled with sharp intelligence.

There was no way around it. "No, I do not renounce my oath."

She twitched again, her eyes shifting to stare behind me. Alex crept forward, sniffing the blood, his lip curling at the bitter scent.

He got too close. She lashed out, pinning Alex to the ground with a claw, her eyes fierce. "Give me your word, Tracker. Free her from them, when you free the human child." Her claws dug into Alex and he cried out, struggling against the impossibly strong claws. Her meaning was crystal clear.

Double fuck.

"I will free her, one way or another," I said.

Her eyes narrowed, understanding exactly what I said, but more importantly, what I hadn't. I would set her sister free, or I would kill her. Either way, the Coven would no longer control the young Harpy.

She withdrew her claws from Alex, who scrambled backwards until he pressed up against O'Shea. "That will do." She coughed and shifted her weight. I couldn't stop the involuntary tensing of my muscles. Even this close to death, she was a deadly adversary, one that could kill me with barely a flick of one claw.

"Do you know why the Coven is stealing children?" After seeing the mineshaft, I had no doubt the kidnappings had been going on for a while, which meant there was more than one kid down there.

The Harpy took a deep rattling breath, the scent of coppery blood on her words as she exhaled. "The Coven tagged us, with this." She lifted a claw and I saw a ruby embedded in the top of her foot.

I bent over and put the edge of a knife to it, popping it free, and slid it into my pocket.

The Harpy blinked twice, eyes un-focusing in between each movement. "That is what you must remove from my sister if you are to free her. My sister's true name, call her by it and she will know you mean her no harm. Eve, her name is Eve." Her chest stilled, and the last of her life escaped from her as she breathed her sister's name. Damn it.

Standing up, I brushed the dirt off my jeans. "Let's go."

O'Shea and Alex climbed into the Jeep in silence, but it didn't last for long.

"I think we should pull up the files on the other three kids that are missing," O'Shea said, his voice steady, considering the last half an hour.

I put the Jeep in gear and headed out, taking a long loop back to the highway. "At this point it doesn't matter. We'll find the other kids when we find India." I tapped the steering wheel with my left hand. "They're looking for something, children with certain abilities. Don't you ever wonder about those cases where kids just up and vanish? They're stolen by people like the Coven. But we're running out of time if we are going to get any of them back."

"Stolen," Alex grumbled from the back.

I glanced back at him to see his lip curling up, and looked back to where I was going. The light started to fade, our day almost done. We would need the cover of night to break into the Coven's stronghold and get India out. And maybe a pile of other kids.

"I wish Milly was with us," I said softly.

"Why isn't she here?" O'Shea asked.

"Sorry, I'm not used to anyone but her riding along with me." I turned back onto the highway and headed into Bismarck. Giselle's place was loaded with gear, ready as my backup stash.

"You didn't answer the question."

My shoulders tightened, and I had to resist the urge to push O'Shea out of the Jeep at high speed. Taking one long, slow breath, I answered him, albeit through gritted teeth.

"Milly's a Witch, a damn good one, but she's finally been accepted into the Coven, which means she can't have contact with anyone outside of the group. In the past, she's gone with me, always been my partner on the hard salvages. The ones I couldn't do on my own."

Silence reigned for all of three seconds. "You've got me, you don't need Milly."

I wanted to bash my head into the steering wheel; it would be less painful than trying to explain a lifetime of knowledge to one oblivious agent who thought he understood. I settled for shouting at said former FBI agent. "YOU AREN'T A WITCH."

"So?"

Unbelievable. The arrogance of some people truly astounded me. Again, I struggled for control; a slight glance at O'Shea stiffened my spine. He enjoyed this back and forth. A smile curved up the edge of his lips and his eyes definitely sparked with humor. The bastard.

Slamming my mouth shut on the response I'd been prepared to assault him with, like how stupid could he possibly be and what was he thinking taking on supernaturals as a human, I swallowed the words down instead.

"You going to go all Ice Queen on me now?"

Alex barked from the back. "Icy Queenie!"

Good grief. Alex's excitement and apparent happiness was infectious, and it took all I had not to laugh out loud.

Biting down on the laughter that bubbled up, I stared at the road, focusing on the need to get to Giselle's and get loaded up. My humor faded. This was going to be a bad hunt; really, really bad. Nothing had gone right so far, and my gut feeling was that it wasn't going to change.

The sky was dark when we pulled into Giselle's yard, and I wasn't expecting company, which was my bad. Lights flicked on, sirens came alive, and we were surrounded by police officers with guns drawn and pointed at us before the Jeep rolled to a stop.

I glared at O'Shea next to me, wishing again it was Milly in the passenger seat.

I hated being right.

20

The processing took about three minutes tops. O'Shea was cuffed and flung into the back of a police cruiser, and I was hauled out to the back of the Jeep for questioning, my hand never leaving Alex's collar. If it came off, everyone would see him for what he was, which would create a shit storm of problems we did *not* need.

From what picked up in the scattered radio squawks I could hear, there was an anonymous tip that O'Shea was with me and we were headed to Giselle's. My gut was telling me that it was the black Coven getting inventive with ways to slow me down. I couldn't prove my theory, but it was the only thing that made sense.

Alex pressed hard against my leg, his teeth chattering, but he had enough understanding of the situation not to say anything. I tried my best to focus on what the officer in front of me said.

"So, you're telling me that Agent Liam O'Shea tracked you down and forced you to drive him . . . here?" The disbelief in the officer's voice told me everything I needed to know. I was about to go down with O'Shea. Two birds, one big nasty, lying stone. There was no way I would be walking away from this.

I let Alex's collar slip through my fingers. "Find Milly." He lifted his big dark eyes to mine and nodded, then took off like a shot into the overgrown and junk-filled alley that ran alongside Giselle's home, much to the dismay of the officers around us. Even though we were at odds, she would look out for Alex, would maybe even come to pull my ass out of this fire. Maybe.

"Oops," I said. "Fingers slipped." The officer glared at me, his face darkening to a shade that, in the light of the sirens, looked a distressing shade of purple.

Unable to help myself, I asked, "Do you have high blood pressure? You look like a plum that's about to explode."

Without further ado, I was spun, frisked and handcuffed with my hands behind my back, then shoved inside the same police cruiser as O'Shea. Or Liam, I suppose.

My hip bumped against his; he glanced over at me, but said nothing. All that spark and humor I'd seen earlier was gone, wiped out. Back were the cold, distant dark eyes I'd grown used to seeing glare at me out of his sharp angled face. There were no handles inside, nothing to even rattle in an attempt to get out. But I wasn't panicking, at least not yet.

Leaning back into the pleather seats, I stared up at the battered ceiling of the cruiser. It looked as though more than one set of feet had been smashed into it. "You never told me your name was Liam."

He said nothing, so I kept talking. "It suits you." I shifted down a little further and put my feet on the ceiling, setting them inside the prints of the previous passenger. "He had big feet. At least a size fourteen or fifteen. Maybe he was a Big Foot." That got his attention.

"They aren't real." No one was in the cruiser with us yet, so I leaned toward him and put my lips to his ear. "You sure about that?"

He shivered and a flash from a camera went off behind us. A picture of me snuggling up to the agent who'd shot his partner while hunting me. Oh, that was not going to help us any.

An officer got in the car, flipped the lights off, and stared at us through the metal bars that kept us from climbing out. "Was she worth it?"

O'Shea glanced over at me, and I smiled up at him and gave him a wink. "Go ahead, tell him the truth." Something in me wanted O'Shea—Liam—to smile again.

There it was; a flicker of devilry in those dark eyes. "I don't know. Yet."

Heat, intense, searing heat flared between us. I couldn't look away—the promise of that one, single, simple word was all it took to spin my mind back to a very tight cramped bathroom and the feel of his chest under my fingertips. The taste of his lips and tongue against mine. I swallowed hard, my heart pounding, blood rushing to places I'd ignored for a long time.

"You're a disgrace, piece of shit cop killer," the officer said, breaking the spell between us.

I looked out my window, feeling the distance between O'Shea and I seemingly shrink. His side pressed up against mine, and I knew my mind hadn't been playing tricks on me.

His hand stole around my back, hampered by his handcuffs, but undeterred. Even if I'd wanted to pull away from him, I couldn't, there was nowhere for me to go. Fingers linking with mine, he leaned into me harder. I stared at his mouth, only inches away from my face, and tried to form a cohesive thought other than how good he tasted.

Then he jabbed his key into my hands. Key? Blinking, I flicked my eyes up to his, which were almost laughing at me. My fingers curled around the key and I slid it into the handcuffs. A small 'snick' of metal unlatching and I was free. In a manner of speaking.

"Now what?" Still crushed up against him, my voice was whisper soft.

"We give them a show, one that'll make them pull over and try to separate us."

"You just want another chance at my lips." My whisper was just a tad too breathy. Damn I sounded eager. Maybe I shouldn't have employed Milly's tactics. They were certainly landing me in a whole different pot of hot water.

His lips quirked up, putting a slight dimple in his cheek. How had I not noticed that before?

He pushed his face even closer to mine, a mere shiver away from touching. "You don't?"

I couldn't think of anything to say that wouldn't damn me all to hell and back, and my own reaction to him did that well enough.

The same officer who'd interrupted us before did so again. Thank the gods.

"You two, chill out." His babyish features pegged him for the rookie he obviously was. That, and the way his hand never strayed from the butt of his gun.

O'Shea obediently slid back to his side of the seat, and I sucked in a large lungful of air. Moments later another officer joined the first and we were off to the police station. Or at least, that was what I thought. About ten minutes into the drive the silence broke.

The young officer turned to his partner. "Where's our escort?"" I thought we were going to be flanked by the FBI?"

In answer, the older cop shook his head. "Pull over."

What was this? The young cop did as he was told, without question, putting the car in park. Not a good thing, even I knew that.

"Shit." O'Shea mumbled under his breath. "Be ready."

For what? I wanted to ask—

The older cop pulled his gun, placed it right against his partner's head and pulled the trigger, the shot reverberating, shaking my eardrums. Blood and brain matter splattered the inside of the cop car in a macabre graffiti. I almost pulled my hands up to my ears, at the last second managing to keep them behind me, hiding the fact they were no longer cuffed.

The older cop's image wavered, and then I stared at one of the ugliest trolls I'd ever seen. Not that any of them are particularly handsome, but he won the 'nasty looks' contest hands down. Orange and yellow spotted skin hung in folds off his body, the clothes he'd been wearing tore and revealed far too much for my taste. His four-fingered hand clutched at the gun and he waved it at us, one eye hanging from its socket, the other blinking rapidly as if to clear some unseen haze.

"Get out," the troll commanded.

I knew there was a reason this would work out in our favor. "Can't, no door handles inside. It's a human thing you know." I shrugged. "You want us out you need to get the door open for us."

Grumbling, the troll smashed the side door to let himself out.

Now it was my turn to be pithy. "Be ready."

"For . . ." O'Shea started to ask when the troll grabbed the door on my side and wrenched it off.

"Get out."

Sliding carefully, slowly, across the seat, I wracked my brain for the best way to handle this. Trolls were sketchy at the best of times. One minute your friend, the next they were trying to eat you alive. This one didn't look to be interested in making new friends. He (and yes it was a he, judging by the way his double genitalia hung nearly to his mid-thigh) glared at us and clicked his broken teeth together, bits of tooth flicking out around him. The only upside I could see was if we had something he wanted, he could be swayed to our side, momentarily at least. Trolls were fickle, and that could work in our favor.

I stepped out of the car. The six-foot tall troll stepped back, his hanging eye staring around as if seeing us for the first time. "You're prettier than they said. Those witches were right; you will be a fun time."

Ugh, that was not what I wanted to hear, not the part about the fun or the fact that he'd been sent by the black Coven. Both of his, um, members started to rise as his hanging eyeball roved up and down my body.

A long, split tongue licked his lips. "I could let you go if you do something nice for me," the troll said, stepping forward.

"No," O'Shea said, stepping around me, putting his body in the line of fire.

"This is not the time to get all white knight on me," I said, keeping my voice low.

The troll snarled and lifted the gun, his finger twitching against the trigger.

Using my hip, I bumped O'Shea out of the way and walked closer to the troll, swaying my body as seductively as I could and batting my eyes, much to his delight, if the way his loose hanging eye lit up was any indication.

"You know, I always wondered what a double whammy would be like," I said.

The troll puffed up his chest, his free hand stroking down the folds of skin that hung from his body to cup one of his overlong members.

I struggled to hold back the gag. That was not attractive in the least, but I kept moving forward, closer to the troll, and the gun he held leveled on O'Shea. Sure, it could backfire, it could explode, hell, it could do all sorts of weird things. But after seeing it blow out that young officer's brains all over the inside of the car, I wasn't going to take any chances.

There was only one weak spot I would be able to reach, and so even though I didn't want to, I sidled up to his hanging bits.

With an exaggerated slowness, I lifted my hand and placed it on the troll's upper chest, massaging my fingers into the loose skin. "Do you know who I am?"

"You're that Tracker, who goes after kids," he said, and I rubbed harder across his collarbone, inching closer to the dangling eye.

The troll rumbled under my hand, the skin vibrating to the point of making it ripple like a bowl of Jell-O that had been shook. He puffed out his chest which stretched the skin, making it taut, the rumbling in his chest now caused a sound reminiscent of a large bull frog's mating call. Gross. I bit back the disgust filling me, making me want to pull away. But I had to get that gun away from him.

Like now.

I reached up and grabbed the eye, squeezing it just short of it popping like a grape in my fingers.

The troll howled and the gun swung toward my head. "Drop it!" I hung onto the eyeball, applying more pressure with one nail.

He screeched, and then a body, O'Shea's to be exact, tackled the troll to the ground, the gun pinned between them. The connective tissue to the eye snapped, the troll screeched again, and I was left standing there with an eyeball in my hands while O'Shea handcuffed the screaming, writhing troll like it was something he did regularly.

Gun secured, O'Shea stood.

I just stared at him. "I had it under control you know."

"I couldn't watch you fondle that thing anymore," he snapped.

My jaw dropped, and I was about to tell him just where he could stick his meddling when a wave of fear hit me that was not my own.

India.

I froze and focused on her. She was terrified and her life force wavered. Shit, shit, shit.

"We've gotta go," I said. "India's in trouble."

O'Shea glared at me. "You say that like it's something new. Like she wasn't in trouble before."

I wasn't about to explain my ability to sense people, certainly not to him. "Get in the car, we've got to get weapons and get back out to the mine shaft. Now."

He started to go around to the driver's side.

"I'm driving," I said, jogging to catch up to him.

Hoisting the body of the young cop out of the seat, O'Shea let out a sharp breath. "Here, just let me move this for you."

The cop's head rolled, exposing what was left of his brains inside the gaping black hole that had blown out the side of his head. Much as I didn't want to admit that it was affecting me, the sight was almost too much. Muscles tensing, I fought against the emotions rising in me. Sorrow for his family, grief for him, and an unmistakable sense of regret that was not my own, but O'Shea's. Damn. I clamped down, forcing the feelings back, and behind that came a bolt of terror that was pure child. India was panicking and that was not a good sign. She had to be the number one priority. I'd thought I had time to prep, but it was obvious that wasn't going to be the case, which meant we were going to go barreling in there with next to nothing.

We slid into the cop car. The blood on the back of my seat, trailing down my left side, was cool, but not yet starting to dry. I put my hands on the wheel, jumping as the radio came to life, the voice static-filled, but still loud.

"Bravo Echo thirty-nine, come in. Over." I turned to look at O'Shea.

"You'd better answer this one, Agent."

He picked up the receiver and answered back. "Bravo Echo thirty-nine. Here. Over."

The response was surprising.

"Please disregard the instructions to bring the prisoners to the main jail; an unmarked will be intersecting with you to take over their transport." The radio clicked off and I shared a look with O'Shea while he answered again in the affirmative before turning off the radio.

"That can't be good," I said. "Why wouldn't they just allow the transport to continue as is?"

"Could be FBI. Could be one of your uglies has taken over."

"Hey! They aren't *my* uglies."

O'Shea blew out a sharp breath and pinched the bridge of his nose. "Whatever it is, it won't be good for us, and certainly not for India."

For once, we were in agreement, though it came a little too late.

I started the police cruiser as two black vans screeched to a halt, pinning us down. I held my breath, expecting more trolls or maybe a golem, but all that poured out of the nondescript vans were humans.

FBI agents covered in riot gear pointed guns and tazers at us, but other than that, I let out a breath. This could be handled.

"They aren't going to let us go after her," O'Shea said, stating what I thought was rather obvious.

"Yup. So you ready to kick some ass and break the law to rescue a little girl?"

He turned his head, his dark eyes holding mine for a brief moment. He didn't say anything. From outside, they shouted at us to get out of the car with our hands up. Of course, that wasn't going to happen.

I placed my foot lightly on the gas pedal, ready to go the second O'Shea gave me the nod. Because I wasn't taking him with me if he wasn't in 100 percent. I didn't need dead weight and worries about the law dragging me down when it came to getting India out alive.

"I'm crossing to the dark side I guess," he said, and that was all I needed.

The car was made for ramming, and even in the tight space between us and the two vans, it did its job.

With my foot hard on the gas pedal, we smashed into the van in front of us first. I shoved it almost out of the way before being forced to throw the car into reverse, but it gave us enough room to spin backwards, do a one eighty and peel away from the underpass.

Bullets ricocheted off the back of the car, and I ducked instinctively.

"Ever lose a tail before?" O'Shea asked.

"Once, but I wasn't in a police car. This isn't exactly a car that's going to blend in you know."

He grunted. "Move over."

"What?"

He was already shifting, sliding across the seats to take my place and forcing me into the passenger seat. My ass rubbed across his upper thighs, and he let out a sharp hiss of air that, in any other circumstance, would have made me think I'd hurt him. Not so much here.

He flipped on the lights and sirens and headed for the freeway. A glance behind showed the two vans were already on us, only a few hundred feet behind. I clicked my seatbelt into place, the possibility of falling out extremely high due to the passenger door hanging by only a half a bolt.

"We need gear, climbing gear." But where the hell were we going to get that kind of stuff now?

"They'll have it in the vans," O'Shea said, cranking the wheel and dodging around a slow moving car.

"You mean in the vans behind us?"

"Yes, along with lights, weapons, and body armor. Those vans are always fully loaded, prepped for anything that might cross their path."

A thought hit me. "Don't lose them. We need what they have."

He barked out a laugh. "Shit, they're exactly what we need."

"I think we have the diversion we need to get past the Harpy and our rigging all in one shot." I stared out the back window as O'Shea dodged in and out of traffic.

The chase, if it could be called that, was pretty sedate in terms of what I was thinking would happen. There were no more gun shots, no car crashes, and no squealing tires. We led, the black vans followed, and no other law enforcement showed up. That alone made me wonder. What if this was the mysterious Arcane Arts division of the FBI? A chill inserted itself into my middle. That would make the most sense, but it also had the biggest ramifications. O'Shea drove and I focused on India. She was alive, terrified, but still with us. As I connected with her, I felt a shard of pain rip through her psyche, one that rolled over into me, stealing my breath away.

"What?" The concern was evident in O'Shea even as he worked to lose the two vans.

"India, they're hurting her," I whispered, the pain making my throat close.

"Are you psychic?"

I didn't answer. Couldn't. I was too busy trying to stem the pain India was being forced to endure. It started as it always did when a supernatural had had enough of being patient. The Coven was trying to break her; make her pliable to their will.

While O'Shea drove, I fought hard to give India the strength she needed. "I'm here," I whispered. "Just hang on a little longer."

It didn't take long for us to be back in the badlands, skidding down side roads and hitting the same bumps Alex had been so excited about earlier. The mineshaft came into view and, hovering above it, was the last Harpy, Eve; her eyes even at this distance glittered with hatred. We'd killed two of her sisters. She had every reason to want our guts on a platter.

The downside was we had no weapons, no spells, and no back up.

The upside? You got it, there wasn't one.

21

The vans were pretty much right on top of us when we spun to a stop. Eve rose into the air above us with a screech. She could have hidden herself from the other humans, but the fact that she didn't told me a great deal about what was going to happen. She planned to kill us all. No witnesses, no need to hide.

I ran around the side of the car and ducked as Eve slammed into the hood, her claws swinging straight for me. Rolling, I dodged the razor-sharp talons, feeling them slice through my leather coat, the rip of the material far too close to the sound of flesh being pulled at for my liking. A hand yanked me back toward the mineshaft as the Harpy launched a second attack.

"Bitch, I'm going to pull you apart, one tendon at a time," she screamed.

There was no doubt in my mind she could do just that, and I wasn't sticking around to watch her try. If I could free her while I got India out from under the Coven's 'loving' care, then I would, otherwise I'd have no choice but to kill her. One did not control a Harpy; not even the spell the Coven had on her would last forever.

O'Shea dragged me over to the mineshaft and we ducked down behind it.

A wave of India's fear hit me hard, buckling my knees. If this kept up, I was going to have to block her completely and I didn't want to do that. Right now, I had the feeling she was only hanging on because she could sense me.

The Harpy rose up in front of us and her body started to buck; puffs of feathers erupted out of her as arrows protruded from her body. Not that it would kill her, she needed a blow from a spelled weapon or another supernatural creature to actually kill her. But the men in the black vans didn't know that.

It was my turn to pull O'Shea down as Eve streaked over the top of us and into the group of—I did a quick count—ten men.

Blood sprayed up in a fountain as an agent's head was ripped off with a single pull from the Harpy's powerful beak. A second followed suit, and then the real bloodbath began. O'Shea and I stood, open mouthed in horror, as the Harpy spelled the men, freezing them where they stood, then eviscerated each of them, letting them slump to the ground to die slow and painful deaths. Her voice sung a lullaby that echoed across the badlands, and the pack of wolves in the distance picked up the harmony. Creepy, beautiful, deadly, and horrifying. There was a sense of loss in her song, the words unrecognizable, but the tune made me think of someone mourning.

O'Shea stumbled forward and I caught his arm. "Oh, no you don't." But it was as if he didn't hear me. Again, he took a step, to go around me, and I put my body directly in his path. "O'Shea, stop!" He didn't listen. I slapped him hard across the face, but there was no response.

"Liam," I said, and he turned to face me, his eyes full of confusion. Taking a deep breath, I slid my hands up over his face. "You can't go to her."

"She's hurting," he whispered. "I don't want her to hurt anymore."

I glanced over at the Harpy; we didn't have much time before she would finish the gore fest and turn her attention back to us. I wasn't so sure calling her by name would be enough to stop her, no matter what her sister said.

I pulled his face down to mine and kissed him, and felt his arms wrap around me after a brief pause. I tried not to think about how good it felt to be held against a warm, hard male body, how much I missed just the simplicity of human contact, how much I didn't really want to let go of him. His tongue explored the inside of my mouth, taking its time tasting me, and I returned the favor, finally pulling back to stare up into those midnight dark eyes. They were clear of her song; the hypnotic effect of her singing gone.

"Did you just save my life by kissing me?" He didn't let go, but held me tighter still against him.

I wanted to believe it was some last remnant of the spell from the Coven, but the way my lower body tightened and my pulse sped up, I knew it was much simpler than that.

I wanted him.

"You know what they say, a kiss a day keeps the Harpy away." I tried for humor, but my eyes slid to

the bloodbath going on. If I'd thought we could have
made a difference, I would've tried to stop her.

"I guess I'd better keep you close then," he said, his
eyes dipping to my lips.

I pushed him back before his arms tightened anymore.

"We don't have time for this." I fought the feelings
he aroused, as well as the guilt washing over me. Here
we were, kissing while men were being eaten by a
Harpy; not what I'd call good manners on our part.

He nodded, his face shutting down, all business
again. Which was good. Really, it was. As I tried to
convince myself of that fact, O'Shea led me around
the side of the van closest to us while Eve dug into the
fresh meat on the ground.

"These vans are equipped for anything, even scaling
buildings."

There was a click when he slid the door open that,
to me, sounded like a shotgun blast, and I spun to
face Eve. But her head was still down, the edges of her
neck covered in blood and intestines as she pulled the
men apart.

I clamped my teeth together, unsure of whether it was
to keep the vomit from spewing up and out of me or to
keep my teeth from chattering. Either way, I had to hold
it together. O'Shea grabbed the rappelling gear, one
harness, and a massive coil of rope. I peeked into the
van. It was chock full of weapons, my kind of weapons.
Blades of all lengths, whips, leather armor, and even a
couple of shields. What the hell? No, there wasn't time
to question this, though I had a sneaking suspicion this
was no coincidence. This was my first real look at the

Arcane Arts division of the FBI. At least they came pre-pared, though their training was sorely lacking.

I pulled down two large blades—one curved, one straight—and settled them on my back in a cross pull holster that sat there as if it were made for me.

I fingered a tag on the leather straps and my breath froze. "This has my name on it."

"What?" O'Shea asked, his eyes scanning the tag. "That . . . doesn't make any sense."

They knew about me. Shit! But why would they have put stuff in my size into their van and then chased us across the badlands? As O'Shea said, it didn't make sense.

India's fear hit me in a wave that collided with my own, spiraling upwards through my body until it was all I could do to keep from screaming. A large pair of hands grabbed my arms and shook me, forcing me to look up into O'Shea's eyes.

"Pull it together, Adamson. I can't do this without you."

More than anything else, that admission snapped me out of it. Later. I would deal with the implications of this later.

Geared up, we crept around the edge of the van. Eve had finished feeding and preened her feathers.

"How are we going to get past her?"'

Now that I had the weapons, I could probably take her on; she was young and inexperienced, scared. Alone. Shaking my head at my own stupidity, I motioned for O'Shea to stay behind the van.

"Let me deal with this," I said, my resolve firming. "You get the harness on. Seeing as there is only one, you will have to pack me down." I told myself Eve was just another child, *just another child*. That mantra spun through my head, but it didn't lessen the fear making my skin clammy.

The Harpy lifted her head, her beak clacking at me. "You are too stupid to even believe. Do you think I won't kill you because I've feasted well?"

Lifting my hands to show her I had no weapons, I shook my head. "No, I expect you won't kill me because your sister asked me to free you, Eve."

She let out a screech, her eyes widening until they were completely dilated, and she stumbled backwards, her wings flapping. "She wouldn't have told you my name." But her voice had lost its edge and she sounded like the child her sister claimed she was. Her emotions swirled toward me, and I let myself feel them. Fear, uncertainty, loss, and pain.

Wiping my hands on my jeans, I tried not to shake as I stepped toward her. Her left foot glittered as she stepped away from me, a blood red ruby catching the light as she walked.

"You'll have to hold still if you want me to remove that," I said, pointing at her foot.

Her feathers trembled, rippling as if there were a breeze blowing, but there was no wind. Just the raw emotions that shook her frame.

Eve said nothing, and I took a steadying breath and pulled one of the swords out. She hissed and raised her wings, her terror filling me. She was afraid of me. Her emotions were raw, an open book, and I knew if I kept tapped into them, I might have the warning I needed if she was going to attack me. Maybe.

Moving slowly, I spoke to help calm her. "I have a pet werewolf you know. His name is Alex. He was from a pack that tried to kill him, and somehow he ended up on my porch one night, bleeding and hurt."

I was a few feet closer, and she lowered her wings. "Why didn't you kill him?"

"I don't like killing. He was scared and needed help. I know how it feels to be in that kind of a bind."

She cocked her head and her eyelids fluttered. "What do you know of fear? You are a Tracker. You are a killer."

My chest constricted. Was that how all the other supernaturals thought of me? As a killer?

"I was accused of killing my baby sister a lot of years ago." I crouched by her foot and put the blade to the edge of the stone, working around it to loosen it up. "She was the first I tried to find, but she was already dead by the time I realized I could track people. No one believed me, not even my parents. I had nowhere to turn to for help." I lifted my eyes to hers. She was crying. "Am I hurting you?" There was no blood from her foot, no cuts from my blade; I was being as careful as I could.

"I miss my sisters. They kept me safe," she said, her head dropping to her thickly feathered chest.

I worked at the stone and with one final pop, it flipped out of her foot, leaving a depression but no wound.

Tucking the stone into my pocket, I stood and backed away. There was no glitter of a spell breaking, no clash of thunder or backlash of power being released. The most powerful of spells were often also the simplest, and this was one of those. "There. You're free of the Coven now."

She twitched and her wings shook. "I have nowhere to go. We are the last of the Harpies in this range; the others would kill me because I am young and alone."

Deadly, they are as deadly as anything out there. But I still opened my damn mouth. "You can stay with me. For a while."

Her eyes flicked up, hope flared between us like a sucker punch to my gut. I'd killed her two sisters and now she was looking at me as if I was her savior. Shit.

I motioned to O'Shea, who made his way to the mineshaft and starting hooking up the gear.

"We have to go. If no one shows up, wait for us here. If people show up, hide yourself,"

She bobbed her head and settled down on the ground. It was too surreal, even for me, to see the sprawled out half-eaten bodies next to the young Harpy I'd just given leave to stay with me.

"What the hell are you thinking?" O'Shea snapped my own thoughts back at me.

"We have to get India. Then I will deal with the rest." I forced the confidence into my voice and my movements; forced myself to turn my back on Eve, though my every instinct screamed at me to *run*.

O'Shea slipped on the harness and climbed up on top of the mineshaft, a glow stick dangling from his hip barely touched the murky darkness below him. He passed me a flashlight, which I stuck in my back pocket.

Then he held out his hand. "Come on."

Tucking away the sword I'd used to pry the gem from Eve's foot, I did as he asked and put my palm against his. He yanked me to his chest.

"Hang on."

"Like I was going to let go?" I lifted my eyebrows in tandem.

He flushed and I snaked my arms around his neck, shifted more to his side before I wrapped my legs around his hip and right thigh. Even though it wasn't a tight squeeze, the mineshaft brushed up against us, banging us back and forth down the pipe, our bodies swaying with the movement of the rope.

O'Shea worked the ropes, lowering us slow and steady, his muscles flexing under his dirty white shirt. At some point along the way he'd lost his tie. His hair was a complete mess and again, I could see just before we lost the light from above that there was a glint in his eye.

"You having fun, Agent?" I tightened my grip on his thigh as the pipe bumped into my hip.

"What?"

"This whole time, with all this crap going on around us, you look like you're enjoying it." The pulse of his blood beat strong against my hands. I forced myself to not trail my fingertips along his neck and jaw, to feel the stubble that had been pressed against my own face not so long ago. I swallowed hard. This close proximity was not a good thing for me. Never in all the times I'd been tracking down kids had I been so distracted, and it wasn't like this was the first time O'Shea had been involved—to some degree—with a salvage I was on. He'd almost always been there on the periphery, just on the edge of my life.

He shifted his arms and we slid down, the light around us dimming completely except for the little glow stick below us. "I don't think enjoying is the right word."

We slid down into the darkness, no longer able to see each other's faces. Maybe that was what made me so damn bold. "Yes, it is. You're enjoying this. Like a kid who's never been to a party before and gets taken to the biggest frat house in town and lets loose. So what gives?"

Silence, except for the creak of the rope, and when he spoke, he went in a totally different direction.

"What really happened to Berget?" His words would have sent me running in a different direction except for the fact that I was stuck with him in a freaking mineshaft that would probably take us another half an hour to get to the bottom of.

It was my turn to be silent. But then, hell, it wasn't like he didn't know anything about the supernatural. I could tell him, I just didn't want to.

"I was watching her for our parents. Berget loved the park, loved being outside. So I took her to the biggest park in the city late in the afternoon, close to dusk." My fingers found the collar of his shirt and I fiddled with it; of course he already knew all this, it was in the files on me and the case, no doubt. "Anyway, when we got there, I had this strange sensation of something not being right. I didn't know what it was, but I told Berget to keep close."

We slid down a few more feet while I gathered my-self. Much as I hated talking about this, I suddenly wanted O'Shea to know completely and irrevocably that it wasn't me who'd killed Berget. But I wasn't going to analyze why it was important to me, as my fingers brushed along the back of his neck.

"There are some people who have blood pulsing through them that is . . ." I tried to find the right word. "Exotic and tantalizing to the supernaturals who drink blood to live."

He kept shifting us lower, but still managed to sound as if we were just going for a walk in the park. "You mean like vampires?"

I nodded, though he couldn't see it. "Yes, and day-walkers, and a slew of other creatures too. I found out after she went missing that Berget had that kind of blood. It sings to the supernaturals, almost demands to be taken in a way. I don't fully understand because it's not something that's a part of me, nor is it a common occurrence. What I know is there are very few people with this kind of blood who make it to adulthood. Very few." And that was the hardest truth about my job as a Tracker. So few of the children were brought home to their families alive.

"So what took her?"

"A pair of vampires." I thought about Doran, how he'd wanted a taste of my blood, and I shivered. Al-though I had no doubt my blood was tasty, I never would have made it to where I was now if I'd carried the same blood as Berget. I'd have been stolen and drained years ago.

"So these vampires took your sister and you couldn't stop them?" His words sliced through me as if it had been only moments since Berget had been killed instead of years.

"I was young and had no training; I didn't know I was a Tracker. It was after Berget went missing that my abilities awakened." And that was the crux of it. If she hadn't been killed, I wouldn't be able to help these other kids. Yet, I'd give them all up to have her back in my life, to have had a family that was whole and not shattered into pieces. It was also a line Giselle had drilled into me as she'd trained me and Milly. I couldn't change the past, but I had to use what it had given me in order to keep Berget's death from being wasted.

Tears traced down my face in the pitch-black darkness, and even though O'Shea kept asking me questions, I couldn't answer them. Not that it mattered anyway. I couldn't change the past, and it was India's life that now lay in the balance.

22

The bottom of the mineshaft was lit, the walls studded with sconces filled with a brilliant purple and red flame.

"What the hell is that?" O'Shea's voice was hushed as he unhooked from the harness.

"Witchlight. It'll last until the maker of it is killed or chooses to extinguish the light for some reason." I pulled out a sword and scanned the area, flicking the flashlight on even though there was plenty of light. The mine itself was good size, tall enough that I couldn't see the ceiling and wider than a four lane highway. Unfortunately, I could just imagine all the nasty creatures needing so much room to maneuver.

First, we had to find the actual crossing point to make it to the other side of the Veil. I glanced over to O'Shea, then handed him the other sword. "Here, you'd better take this."

He took a few practice swings; his form was pretty good. In fact, his last swipe was a move only some who trained with blades would know. I frowned at him, and he shrugged.

"I started to take lessons once I realized you only carried knives and swords. Figured I might have to fight you one day."

Damn, his foresight was going to serve me well. Even if he'd only learned so he could kick *my* ass. For some reason, the thought made me smile.

There were three options as to which direction to take, but only one tunnel was lit with Witchlight. I pointed with my sword. "Follow the freaky purple light."

O'Shea followed me, letting me lead without an argument. Which was good, all things considered. We needed to be quiet, subtle, and ideally break in and out with India without being noticed. If I could have crossed my fingers I would have, but as it was, I kept my hopes high and my eyes wide open.

From a distance, I picked up the sounds of voices—arguing voices carrying through the cavern as though they were much closer than they actually were.

"You said we could be together this way," a woman said, her voice cracking. "I left my family's Coven for you!"

"It's temporary. We have to see how this Coven operates. Stop being so fucking whiny. It's your goddamned fault we got kicked out of the circle and stuck on guard duty. Stupid bitch." Her male companion snapped at her.

"Nice guy." I muttered.

There was nowhere to hide, so we stepped back behind the slight curve we'd just come around. Again, I didn't need to say anything, O'Shea just followed my lead. Maybe he wasn't Milly, but he did seem to have some redeeming points.

We crouched against the rough cut wall. The cool water dripping down the sides slipped along my arm to drop off the edge of my hand, which gripped my sword. I motioned slightly to O'Shea. He was to go high, I'd go low. The barest flicker of his eyelids told me he understood.

Flowing green robes spun into view and I struck hard and fast, the borrowed blade slicing through the flesh of the female Coven member's stomach and pinning her to the ground. I heard a grunt above me to see O'Shea dispatch the other Coven member, a man dressed in a red silk shirt and black pants that had been stuffed into tall boots.

The woman whimpered and lifted her hands— I knew a spell prep when I saw it. Dropping to my knees, I straddled her chest and pinned her hands above her head. "Hold these for me, would you?" I turned to look over my shoulder. O'Shea's face was grim, but he nodded and stepped around us to put his hands over the woman's wrists.

I ignored O'Shea's frown. "Where is the entrance?"

She shook her head. "I can't tell you."

I let out a sigh. "Your man is dead and you're going to follow in his nasty-ass footsteps if you don't tell us how to get across the Veil. Now where's the entrance?"

She blinked large blue eyes up at me, as if she could con me into letting her go with a few bats of her eyelashes—no doubt, it had worked for her in the past. Reaching down, I pulled the sword out of her stomach and she let out a gasp. Before she could say anything, O'Shea's hand clamped over her mouth. I didn't know whether to be happy or freaked out that he knew what was going to happen. Steeling myself, I pulled a short knife from my boot and jammed it into the wound, pushing until I could feel the resistance of one of her internal organs, a kidney by the location of it. "Tell me now where the entrance is." I banked on the notion she wasn't accustomed to torture.

She struggled, her eyes full of fear and pain. I had a hard time feeling bad for her when I thought of how many kids this Coven had stolen. No, I wouldn't feel bad. I forced myself to push harder, popping through the organ's walls, until her eyes rolled back in her head and she passed out.

"Now what?" O'Shea's eyes bored into mine.

I refused to look away. "We wait for her to come around, and then ask again. We need the exact entrance or we'll walk right past it." I wasn't yet ready to explain what crossing the Veil entailed. Nor did I want to try and explain that he probably couldn't cross with me and would be left behind.

It took longer than I wanted, and each passing minute brought us closer to facing down another member of the Coven, one that wouldn't necessarily be so easy to take down or be taken by surprise. We'd lucked out that these two were having a lover's quarrel.

Another minute passed and she came around, though she tried to hide it. I leaned forward and whispered into her ear. "Unless you want me to puncture and scramble each piece of the rather necessary equipment your body contains, I suggest you tell us where the entrance is." She nodded, her face white and shocky with blood loss. My stomach turned and I fought with the nausea rising in me. The warmth of her blood on my hands, the pulse of life I could feel because my hand was partially inside of her. Not a good time to want to puke. I bit down hard on the inside of my cheek, the pain helping me steer my thoughts away from what I was doing.

Her whisper was just loud enough to be heard over the thrumming of my own blood as it filled my ears.

"The break in the rock. That's the entrance." Her eyes flicked toward the way she and her lover had come. "You're the Tracker."

I nodded. She took a breath and smiled up at me. "They will kill you."

I shrugged and smiled back at her, knowing the smile was anything but nice. "Everybody says that."

Rolling her onto her stomach, we used the belt her boyfriend was wearing to tie her up and placed her around the corner where we'd hid, gagging her mouth for good measure.

"That's all it takes to deal with a witch?"

O'Shea's question made me want to laugh out loud, but I contained it. "Weak ones are incapable of doing magic without their hands." I wiped the blood off my own hands using her skirt. Her head lolled and she groaned, but it was the best she could do. I shrugged off the guilt and turned toward the direction of the crossing.

Again, O'Shea followed me, and I wondered at his willingness to let me lead. A quick look over my shoulder showed him gripping his sword lightly, his eyes never resting in one area for too long.

Three more corners through the Witchlight tunnels and the crack in the wall was right in front of us. It didn't glow, and in fact, looked a lot like all the other cracks we'd passed, except it was wide enough we could have walked in shoulder to shoulder without bumping the walls—and the Witchlight didn't penetrate it. That was the clincher.

"This is it." Now came the really hard part. Making him stay behind without having him throw a fit and without having to explain what crossing the Veil meant.

"O'Shea. Let me look in first, then I'll give you the okay."

He ducked his head inside the crack before I could stop him. "There isn't anything, just a slab of rock." He reached out and tapped said slab with his sword. That would make this easier. O'Shea didn't have any natural ability to cross the Veil, at least not without help.

"Go check down there." I pointed to another tunnel off the main branch, one that didn't have any light going down it, handing him the flashlight. "I'll backtrack and see what I can find, maybe we missed something."

I watched him walk away, his sword raised as if it were a gun. The flashlight held at the handle gave him lots of light as he stepped into the tunnel.

Two strides and I was inside the crack I knew was the entrance I needed. Squinting my eyes, I looked past what this side of the Veil showed me and got a good look at what was really there. A doorway painted a deep maroon and boasting a large lock stood between me and India. I tried the handle, knowing before I did that it wouldn't be so easy. It didn't move, not even a slight jiggle. Fuck, why was I not surprised?

Putting one hand against the door, wishing I could just bust through, I considered my options. One, I could try to force it, using my sword as a hammer on the lock. But this wasn't one of my swords Milly had spelled for me, so it was unlikely it would hold up to that kind of abuse. Two, I could try to figure out the spell they had locking this down, but again, without Milly helping, that would be impossible. Unless there was an even simpler solution than that. More mundane.

"Keys," I muttered. There had to be a key somewhere.

Like on the two Coven members we'd dispatched.

Bolting out of the crevice, I ran back to where we'd left them. The woman was still breathing, but I doubted she'd have the key on her. He was the one in control of things; that much had been obvious. A quick frisk of his pockets and I had a small key palmed, a feeling of relief coursing through me.

"Hang on, India, just a little bit longer," I whispered as I ran back to the crack in the wall. Slipping in, I put my hand on the door.

His flashlight didn't give as much light as he would have liked, and the mineshaft was darker than anything he'd ever dealt with before. If he'd had his way, they wouldn't have separated, but on this front, Adamson knew what she was doing, and for the first time in his life he was starting to trust his partner.

Wow. Trust and partner in the same sentence; how had that happened? And with Adamson, of all people? There was no longer the driving lust he'd felt from the spell, though he could admit she was a beautiful woman; now it had more to do with her dedication to finding this kid, even when the case was so obviously similar to her little sister's. She didn't get distracted by anything. Once she decided a kid needed rescuing, even he and the FBI couldn't deter her. That was worth something to him. Not to mention she had saved his ass a number of times already.

Something on the wall caught his eye. Lifting his sword and light up, he was shocked at the symbols etched into the stone; and it wasn't just one, it was hundreds. Chills swept him, a visceral response to something his body knew was dangerous. Deadly.

She had to see this.

"Adamson?" O'Shea called out softly.

I cringed as his voice echoed through the cavernous space. "Here." I didn't want him to get suspicious.

"I think I found something."

What the hell? He couldn't have found anything, unless . . .

"It's a trap!" I spun on my heel and ran toward his voice. Shit, I hadn't even considered he'd be able to set off booby traps. They should have been keyed only to supernaturals, one of which he definitely was not.

I sprinted toward the tunnel I'd sent him down, cursing myself for my idiocy. I should have checked first, should have made sure it was safe. His death would be on my shoulders.

Breathing hard, I sped toward the small pinprick of light I could see, knowing it would be too late.

O'Shea turned to face me as I skidded to a stop in front of him, fear making me sweat more than the run, my face damp with perspiration. He looked okay, the planes of his face were sharpened by the way the light hit him, but I didn't see any wounds, no gaping holes or the smell of spells being prepped.

He motioned to the wall, not noticing I was totally freaked out, for which I was grateful.

"Check this out; do you know what it means?" He shone the flashlight on the wall.

I sucked in a large gulp of air. It was a hieroglyph that looked eerily like the pictures India had been drawing all her life. There were stick figures, their bodies neither male nor female, surrounded by orbs. As O'Shea followed the picture's progression with the flashlight, the orbs grew more and more numerous until they completely covered the stick people.

I could guess at what it meant, but didn't really want to. Seeing it like this and not in a child's colourful crayon drawings made me re-think what exactly was going on. Possession was an ugly thing, and if those orbs weren't the kind and loving souls of those who'd gone on before us, then they were the souls who'd been cast down into darkness and were looking for a second chance.

"It's bad. That's what it is." I suddenly didn't want to cross the Veil without O'Shea at my side. It had been a long time since I'd been really afraid, but the idea of being possessed, or dealing with people who were possessed, was a hard one for me to swallow.

"Come on, I found the way in." I jogged back the way we'd come. He followed and I felt him pause as I headed toward the crevice in the wall.

"What are you doing?"

"You have to trust me. This is the entrance," I said, slipping into the crack.

He followed right on my heels. "You were going to go in without me." His accusation hit the mark, but I didn't flinch.

"You have no idea what this all is, the supernatural is something you don't understand, which makes it dangerous not only for you, but me and India." My anxiety grew and it was apparent in my voice. This was taking too long. At any moment, we could be dealing with more of the Coven members, looking for their missing people. "If you're going to come with me, you're going to do what I say, when I say it. Got it, Agent O'Shea?"

Jaw clenched, he gave a curt nod, but said nothing.

Letting out a breath, I turned my back to him and put my hand on the lock he couldn't see. "Hang on to me, and close your eyes until I tell you otherwise."

His hands grabbed the waistband of my jeans, fingers brushed against my spine. I fit the key into the lock and turned the handle, the mechanism clicking as it unlatched, but otherwise it was quiet.

I stepped through, O'Shea tight behind me, his hand not loosening on my jeans. The Veil shimmered around me and I glanced back at O'Shea. His eyes were dutifully closed, but his face twisted in a grimace like he'd smelled something bad. I took one more step, which pulled him all the way across and his face eased as did my tension.

Reaching back, I loosened his fingers. "You can open your eyes."

He did, and I took the opportunity to look around myself. The thing with crossing the Veil was you never knew where exactly you were going to end up. Today, it looked as though we were in a medieval castle. Carved stone walls partially covered with expensive tapestries and oil paintings. Other than that, I couldn't tell *where* exactly we were. For all I knew, we were in England or France.

"Where . . ." O'Shea started to ask.

I lifted a finger to my lips. Reaching for India, I could feel her life force stronger than ever, pulsating with a steady rhythm that would have given me hope if not for her lack of emotion. She was alive, but no one was home.

Pressing up against the wall, I skirted the edges of the room. I didn't have to look back to know O'Shea would be doing the same.

Now that I was on the same side of the Veil as India, I could pinpoint her with ease. Following the pull of her life force, I jogged, wanting to get to her as fast as possible. Distracted by my concern for her lack of emotions, I wasn't paying attention as I should have been; took a sharp right and ran straight into the back of a tall, cloaked figure.

I had a moment of uncertainty, back pedaling as if I could take back my blunder, putting distance between us.

The figure turned; his face only partially visible in the light flickering around us. He looked like someone I knew, or had known a long time ago. Eyes that spoke of pain and suffering, yet light and beauty also captured their azure depths.

"Well, Rylee, it seems the Coven was right. You did turn up after all." His voice was smooth, and I had images flashing through my mind of black satin bedsheets, rose petals, and crisp white wine. I struggled against his hold on my mind. Except for the Unicorn, no one had been able to turn my gifts on me before. Yet, while I'd had no doubt the Unicorn meant me no harm, this man could hurt me without a single moment of lost sleep.

Something pulled me back and I blinked, unaware I'd been slowly moving toward those blue eyes and hypnotizing voice.

"Adamson, focus!" A growl rumbled in my ear, O'Shea pulling me back to myself.

With a speed that surprised even me, I whipped my sword up, pressing the point into the hollow of the cloaked man's throat.

He lifted his hands as if he meant no harm. The bright slash of a silver ring on his left hand caught the light as he moved. "I won't try to stop you; go rescue the child if you want. It's of no consequence to me."

My mouth was dry. "Who are you?" Not that it mattered, not to India, but I had to know.

He smiled, the edges of his lips creeping up over a glimpse of white teeth. "I don't think I'll tell you. Not today. Rylee."

A shiver rippled through me; my name on his lips made me want to throw my clothes on the floor, and writhe naked against him. Trembling, I fought the urge, but again, it was O'Shea who snapped me out of it.

"Let's go." The agent shoved me in the back, jabbing at my spine to prod me forward and around the man who'd so fully caught me in his snare. That thought was what it took to drive me out of my stupor.

I didn't dare look back as we rounded a corner. "Is he following us?"

O'Shea checked and turned back to me, shaking his head. "He's gone. What the hell was that?"

I shivered all over, my body and mind a mass of confusion. "I don't know."

I placed my hands on my thighs and leaned forward, swallowed hard on the fear and confusion attempting to choke me, struggled to get a hold of myself.

O'Shea grabbed my arms and stood me upright. "You can't lose it now. We're too close and we have to get the kid out of here. So pull your shit together and move."

Clenching my fists, I gave him a sharp nod. He was right, there was nothing I could do about that man, and if he wasn't going to stop us, then I didn't need to worry about him.

India was close, only a few doors down. I strode in that direction, pausing in front of the door. There was something bothering me besides my reaction to the man in the cloak.

"Where the hell is everyone?" I hardly realized spoken out loud.

"I wondered the same thing. This is not good." He strode to the far side of the hallway and checked it. "For now, I say we take it as a good sign, don't poke the sleeping bear unless you have to," O'Shea said, keeping his voice low.

"Fine, then shut it." I growled the words at him. I knew he was right, but that didn't mean I should just run through the halls like we were in a daisy-filled field with bright sunshine and butterflies. But something was off, and because I couldn't pinpoint it, my skin itched with the feeling.

A low hum started to fill the air around us, coming from inside the room, which made the itch I already had turn into a knot of nerves.

"This is not good," I said, putting my hand on the door, discovering the dark wood paneling was hot under my hand. India was in the room, I knew that much, but suddenly I knew why we hadn't seen anyone else. The hum of multiple voices filled the air, confirming my worst fear.

India was about to be possessed by a demon.

23

A shuffle down the hall behind us was the only warning we had before a woman stepped around the corner, her hands lifted as she prepped a spell. I lunged at her, my blade catching her just in the crook of her left elbow, slicing deep down to the bone. I followed up the slice with a kick to her hip. She dropped to the floor, and I pinned her head down with my foot. Of course, it would have all been good if she'd been the only one.

"Let her go, Rylee."

Blinking, I turned to look into Milly's face, her eyes hard as she held a deadly spell just inches from my nose. I could see the black spiral of the death magic quivering in her hand, but even so, I had a hard time putting two and two together. O'Shea moved up beside me, a steady presence that helped me get my bearings. Of course, both Milly and I knew the spell would likely dissipate around me. But the other woman, who was nodding at Milly, didn't know that.

The woman under my foot snorted a laugh. "You heard her. Let me go."

I lifted my foot. "Milly . . ."

She raised her hand, black energy sparking with the movement, the threat clear. This had to be a show for the other woman, there was no other explanation.

It took everything I had to step away from the witch I'd injured. India, That was what we had to focus on.

"They're going to let a demon possess India if we keep standing here." My emotions finally starting to shut down. I could be cold, hard, just like I needed to be. A whimper caught my attention and peeking around the corner was a familiar pair of amber eyes.

"Milly mean," Alex whimpered, and my heart broke a little to see my own pain reflected in his eyes.

"Stay there," I said, not wanting him anywhere near what was about to happen.

Milly stepped up to the door and the other witch let her lead.

O'Shea lifted an eyebrow at me, and I shook my head.

My used-to-be best friend put her hand on the knob and twisted, yanking the door open. A blast of energy swirled out, and I didn't think. I just moved, jumping across the gap and pulling Milly out of the way.

A massive crash resounded through the castle as the wall directly behind where we'd just been standing melted into a puddle of molten rock, bubbling and slithering toward us.

I yanked Milly to her feet while she glared at me, but all I could see was the child sitting in the center of a pentagram carved into the floor, her body naked except for the blood that had been poured over her.

"O'Shea!" I bolted into the room, registering the faces of the black Coven. Surprise, anger, and fear mingled with a sense of evil so heavy I actually stumbled right before I reached the auburn-haired little girl, her hazel eyes wide and dilated. The smell of opium was heavy on the air, as was the scent of something akin to road tar, which I knew could be only one thing: demons. Seeing the vacant look in India's eyes, I understood why I couldn't get a bead on her emotions; they'd drugged her. At least, that's what I was hoping.

A blur of a sword and large male body charged up behind me, deflecting blows, keeping me safe as I reached for India, trying to pull her off the pentagram without actually stepping on it myself. Which would be bad, like really bad.

"Get down!" O'Shea's warning came a split second too late. One of the black Coven members physically slammed into me and spun me out toward India, right into the pentagram.

"Two is always better than one," he laughed, as fear spiked through me.

The last thing I saw before hitting the pentagram was Milly battling with three witches, two men and a woman, and O'Shea to one side of me, blood seeping through his white shirt. Then I hit the floor.

The demon trying to possess India had been invisible to me while I was outside the confines of the pentagram, but inside was a different thing. It was shaped like a large ant, with multiple limbs, but stood upright like a human, balancing on a tail that was far too reminiscent of a scorpion for my liking.

I looked down. My body lay prone on the floor, my hand around India's bare ankle.

"We are here in spirit," the bare whisper of a voice said. India's spirit crouched behind her sitting body. "We can't get away."

Swallowing my fear, I cracked my knuckles and faced the demon. "That isn't true. We just have to send this ugly bug butt-face packing. Then we can leave." I gave her a wink, turning my back on the demon for a split second, which I knew better than to do, but I needed to reassure her. Even if I was wrong.

The demon grabbed me around my upper body and lifted me into the air. No weapons on me, I kicked out, catching it in the thorax. There was the crunch of cartilage and the demon dropped me to the ground. There was hope yet; if I could hurt it, then I could kill it. A second kick drove my foot into its chest, forcing it back a step.

"Our master wants to speak with you," it said, mandible clicking back and forth. "You will be rewarded greatly for coming to him of your own free will."

Three more successive kicks and finally the thing stumbled back. "Nope, not interested." Grabbing the closest appendage, I twisted hard, breaking it clean off, a spurt of clear liquid shooting out toward me, hitting me in the face. I swiped off the clear goo, gagging on the scent of rotting meat assailing my nose. Fuck, that was nasty.

Blinking, I caught the movement a second before it struck—the scorpion tail lifted high, then shot toward me with a blinding speed. I rolled to the left, stumbling over my own body. The stinger came down, burying itself into my prone form. That couldn't be good, but there was nothing I could do about it now.

The demon jerked its stinger out and advanced on me. Dodging and ducking, I managed to keep the stinger from hitting me, but there wasn't a lot of room.

"Put the stinger into the pentagram!" Milly shouted, distracting me.

I didn't ask how she could see the demon, but I took her at her word.

The demon's mandible chattered, its frustration coming through and its attacks redoubled. The stinger flew toward my face at a speed I could barely dodge. Sweat rolled down my face when a black blur leapt onto the pentagram, a snarl on his misshapen lips.

"Mean to Ryleeeeeeeee!" He howled as he hit the demon from behind, his teeth sinking into the creature's neck, snapping the head off completely.

Dropping to all fours, white goo covering his muzzle, the werewolf looked down at his paws and the demon's dying body twitching beside him. "No more mean to Rylee. Only good."

"Rylee, the demon, before it fades—use the tail or you'll be trapped!" Milly screamed, her words followed by a thud I didn't want to analyze. Grabbing the demon's tail, I jammed the stinger into the pentagram. A bright burst of light shattered around us; the barrier that had held us inside the confines of the pentagram vanished. I let out a groan, my body and spirit once more attached, a large furry body covering mine, pinning me to the ground. Where the stinger had gone into my physical body from the spirit plain we'd been on, there was a dull throb, but thankfully nothing more. "Alex, get off."

He crawled away from me, but not too far. I sat up to see the battle still raged. "Help O'Shea," I said to Alex, who bounded off after the agent, taking a witch out at the knees in the process.

I scrambled over to India and scooped her into my arms, the buzz of holding the missing child I'd connected to giving me a burst of energy. I slipped off my shirt and put it on her, covering her body. Shy hazel eyes lifted to meet mine. "I knew you'd come for me. I saw you, in a dream."

I nodded, not really understanding why I'd connected so strongly with her over any of the other children I'd sought out. "Come on, kid. Let's get you out of here."

Thanking the heavens we'd made it in time, I started us toward the open door. "O'Shea, Alex, let's go, the party's over."

A quick glance showed there were only two members of the black Coven left standing, and both were engaged with Milly. I wanted to stop and help her, but knew that not only would she not appreciate my help, but she might just turn on me completely.

O'Shea was sweaty, his breath coming in big gulps, but again, his eyes glittered. Yup, he really liked this action-packed life I led. I couldn't stop the snort that escaped me.

"What?"

Clutching India to me, I ignored O'Shea. "Hang on, kid," I said into her hair. She smelled of baby powder and blood. One more person's innocence down the drain of life.

I turned my back on Milly, did my best not to see her strain to keep the two Coven members from her, watched in anger as her own Coven member stood aside and let her fight on her own.

"You aren't going to help her, are you?" I asked, already knowing the answer.

"You have the child, I suggest you leave." The woman I'd bled answered me in a tone that brooked no argument. Except, I wasn't real well-known for backing down from an argument.

"What, you planning to kill her and blame it on the black Coven?" As the words escaped my mouth, I knew that was the truth of it, saw it flash in her eyes.

I put India down. "O'Shea . . ."

"Go save your friend."

A half-smile was all I could manage. Pulling my sword, I ran toward the woman who would be Milly's death if I walked away.

24

Milly dispatched the last two black Coven members and dropped to her knees. The exhaustion was plain on her face. I knew her, and she was completely wiped out. Her "friend" stood over her, hands lifted, and her back to me. Perhaps she thought I was the lesser threat— that was about to be her final mistake. Milly didn't even try to fight back, didn't even twitch with her Coven member prepping a death spell over her head.

It gave me the perfect shot. The witch turned at the last second and tossed a spell at me, fire tingled down the blade of my sword and onto my arm, purple and deadly, but it disappeared in a puff. Her eyes widened. "That cannot be."

"Bitch, you ain't seen nothin' yet," I said. I swung hard and true, removing the woman's head, her mouth an 'O' of surprise that stuck with her even in death. Her head rolled away from us to land where the pentagram was still etched into the floor, right where the demon had died. That seemed fitting.

"You okay?" I crouched in front of Milly.

She started to cry. "They *are* trying to kill me. You were right."

Without another word I wrapped my arms around her shoulders and hugged her tight. "They have to go through me first, you know that."

Her sobs shook her tiny frame and I thought about all the nights I'd listened to her tell me how great the Coven would be once she was a part of it. How life would be good. How much she would learn.

I pulled her to her feet, keeping one arm around her waist. I was tired too, but I hadn't just fought off nearly a dozen witches and survived.

"I'm so sorry, Rylee," she said, her head hitting my shoulder.

"Don't worry about it now. But don't think I won't kick your ass later."

She laughed and then sniffed. "Let's get out of here."

O'Shea picked up India and she clung to him. It was an image that stopped me in my tracks. An auburn-haired child in his arms made me think of things I couldn't have and shouldn't want.

"What's wrong?" Milly lifted her head from my shoulder.

Clearing my throat and scrubbing at my eyes, I motioned at O'Shea. "We need to switch. Give me India, you take Milly."

He didn't question me, just made the swap and we started back toward the door. Milly lifted a hand, stopping us. "The way you came in is swarming with cops. We need to go out the back door."

She directed us deeper into the castle, to the top of a stairwell that was pitch black, narrow, and filled with the scent of urine, feces, and death.

Alex grumbled. "Stinks."

"Buddy, you got that right," I said, taking shallow breaths.

"At the bottom is the cells where they kept the children," Milly said, her voice choking up.

Kept, as in past tense. Shit.

It was India though who spoke next, surprising me, her voice steady despite the words. "They killed all the other kids."

My arms tightened around her instinctively. I couldn't help it. "Do you know how many?"

Her little shoulders shrugged. "I think there were at least three others. One cried all the time, then there was the boy next to me, his name was Jake, and there was another one kid on the other side of me, but that one didn't say anything. Ever." As she spoke, her eyes grew wide and dilated.

I shared a glance with O'Shea over her head. Three kids. The other three missing kids.

I tucked her head into my shoulder. "Okay. Try not to think about it."

"We have to come back for them," O'Shea said.

Of course we did; I wasn't in the habit of letting kids stay missing, not if I could take them home to their parents, even if they were no longer alive. Closure was closure, plain and simple.

We stepped into the dark stairwell, the only light O'Shea's flashlight that faded and flickered every time he brought it close to Milly. It was good enough, though even I jumped a few times at the shadows when they'd flicker and dance on the walls.

"Don't worry, we disabled all the booby traps ahead of time," Milly said.

That explained it. "Before you even got here?"

"I knew you'd be ahead of us, so I convinced the Coven to disable all the dangers far enough in advance that no unsuspecting human would stumble into them."

"But you know that isn't possible. No human would have stumbled into them."

There was a rustle of cloth, and then O'Shea put Milly down. She looked over at me. "They have stayed so secluded that they don't even know how their magic relates to the human world anymore."

My brain struggled to wrap around the thought. To be so close-minded that you weren't even aware of how your magic interacted with others was beyond ridiculous, it was potentially a death sentence.

The five of us crossed the Veil with no problems, going from a dark and cool cave to blinking from the harsh sunlight burning down on us. A sneaking suspicion filled my mind. "Where are we?"

"New Mexico," Milly answered. "Not too far away from where your friend's bar is."

"Son of a bitch, that damn fucking Doran screwed me over!" I trembled to think how much faster I'd have been able to get to India, would have maybe even saved those other kids, if he'd given me this location instead of the roundabout way. There would have been no need for the climbing gear, or battling the Harpies.

Milly touched my arm, took India from me and tucked her into the camouflage Hummer that was parked next to the cave. "Don't think about what might have been. We got India out. That's what matters, remember?"

I stalked over to the Hummer and scrounged around inside, finding several blankets, then went back to gather up the remains of the other kids. O'Shea tried to come with me, but I shook him off. "No, stay here with Milly and India."

"And if you run into that cloaked guy? What then?"

Out of the corner of my eye, I saw Milly perk up, and I angled my body to block her view.

I tried for nonchalant and failed. "I'll run away. Really fast."

He snorted and turned his back on me, which shouldn't have bothered me, but it did. I refused to analyze the simple truth of the matter, but I was starting to trust the ex-agent. My heart swirled with emotions. So much had happened in the last couple days that even I, who was used to this sort of shit going down, struggled with it.

Moving quickly, I slipped across the Veil and back into the castle's dungeon. The first two kids were so small, curled up in fetal positions as they hid from the death that claimed them, that I easily wrapped them in a single blanket. So frail and tiny with weight loss, they were no burden to pack out together, and I did my best not to think about the pain of their deaths, or how much their parents missed them.

On the next trip, I went to the cell I quickly realized held Jake, India's friend. On his shirt he had a nametag, sewn in over the right side of his chest, a soccer ball underneath it. He was still in his soccer gear from when he'd been snatched. Tall socks, cleated shoes, and bright green shorts were his uniform. He looked as if he was just sleeping, with a tousled head of blonde hair.

Crouching down, I took a deep breath, ignored the smells, and reached out for him with my ability, hoping that maybe there was a flicker of life in him still.

Pain shot through me and I fell over on my ass, shocked. He was still alive!

Scrambling, I rushed to his side, gently feeling for a pulse. Nearly a minute passed and then . . . there . . . a beat of his heart. Wrapping him up in the blanket, I stood and headed toward the door, my heart soaring. Little Jake was alive and we were going to keep him that way.

A shuffle of cloth and a flicker of movement to my left made me spin and crouch, peering into the darkness. Body thumping with adrenaline, I stared into the darkness. Nothing. O'Shea's words had put me on edge; I was hearing things, though now I wished I'd taken him up on his offer.

Tension filled the air and I faced the area the noise had come from, backing toward the crossing point.

I reached the doorway leading into the New Mexico desert and stepped through. "Jake's alive!"

Milly and O'Shea ran toward me. Milly would be able to keep the boy alive until we got to a hospital. She couldn't heal him, but she could buy him some time.

"Go, get him in the Hummer!" I stepped away from the cave's entrance and shoved the boy into Milly's arms.

Alex sat next to the Hummer, his eyes snapping wide as he stared over my shoulder, teeth bared. I spun, trying to dodge whatever it was behind me, but couldn't evade the hands that grabbed my waist and jerked me back across the Veil.

25

Sliding back through the Veil, I fought hard against the hands, kicking out, striking with my elbows and fists, but what I hit was so solid there didn't seem to be any response to my blows.

As my body was once more fully on the other side of the Veil, I was flung deep into the dungeon, well over twenty feet. The stone floor was not forgiving when I slammed into it, landing on my right hip. Rolling, I scrambled to my feet to face the one who'd pulled me through.

Or should I say, what pulled me through. A hulking shape stood between me and the entry point to the cave. It was over eight feet tall and while it had arms, legs, and a body, it was not human. Too big, too strange of a shape. Like a puzzle that had its pieces jammed together, despite not really fitting. I couldn't even tell what kind of supernatural it was. Like some sort of supernatural mutt, it didn't fit in anywhere.

Milly's voice echoed through to me. "Rylee?"

"Stay there, it's between us." What 'it' was, I wasn't sure exactly. But it was big enough that it filled the space up from floor to ceiling, and its long arms dangled to the floor with thick muscled hands. In the shadows, it was hard to see just what the skin color was, or any distinguishing marks, other than the fact that it was dark, stunk, and had a menace to it that I could feel vibrating between the two of us. I pulled my sword and advanced on the creature.

"Come on, big boy, you don't really want to stop me from crossing the Veil, do you?" My voice was as sugary sweet as I could manage.

It leaned forward, its face coming into a slant of light from the single flickering wall sconce. There were no eyes, no nose, just a mouth—one that dripped with slime and had very sharp teeth. I steadied myself for a charge, prepped to dodge around the hulking beast and duck back through the Veil. But it just held its ground and didn't move, though at least it didn't advance, either.

I shifted my grip on my sword, prepping for a fight, and in that split second, it attacked.

I'd heard the term greased lightning, but had never truly seen it. The beast, as big as it was, slid past my guard and slammed me into the wall. Thick hands pinned my arms to the stone. My head clunked backwards, and no matter how I struggled, I couldn't loosen the grip. The last of the stitches in my arm ripped out and blood trickled down my arm.

"Come on." This was it? The end of Rylee Adamson would come at the mouth of some unknown, unnamed beast? But it didn't end my life, didn't even try to bite me. Just held me tight against the wall.

Light bloomed over its shoulder and the now familiar cloaked figure stepped out of the shadows. Icy blue eyes perused me with leisure.

"You and your friends have quite the knack for trouble, Ms. Adamson. But all that aside, you and I need to chat." He paused in the middle of lifting his hand to his cowl. "May I call you Rylee? It seems to me we are about to become far more acquainted than what one would think relegated us to last names."

Panic is a bad thing in my profession—it causes loss of life faster than any other emotion—and it rapidly coursed through me. He'd spelled me in a matter of moments before. I closed my eyes and centered myself.

A hand brushed along my cheek. "So soft," he murmured, his voice close enough that I could feel his breath against my skin. The beast holding me did nothing, and I did the only thing I could think of. I reached out to it, connecting with its emotions.

Confusion, fear, loneliness.

Anger.

Bingo. I let it feel my anger, let it feed off my emotion, pushing my fear into it until I felt the spell holding it under the cloaked man's control crack.

Hands that had been holding me tight clenched and my bones creaked under the pressure, but I grit my teeth and tried to remain still.

"Rylee, look at me." His voice triggered something visceral in me. Fear and lust, a powerful aphrodisiac that spiraled upward. The pain in my arms increased, though, and it curbed whatever spell the man was trying to cast on me. I kept my eyes closed. "No, thanks. I like my soul where it is."

"I'm not a thief of souls. You intrigue me; you aren't like any of the others. Not a witch, not a vampire, not a werewolf. But you have such talent." His lips brushed against my ear, the soft inhale of breath sending shivers through me. With everything I had, I shoved emotion into the beast, letting my panic infect it—or at least, that's what I'd hoped for. Milly would come for me. O'Shea wouldn't leave me here.

"I've blocked the entrance; your friends will not be coming for you," he said, as if he were reading my mind, which only heightened my fear. "Do you know I was the one who gave the child the ability to reach you? That I was the one to suggest the date and the park to steal her from? I knew you would follow her here no matter what, and with the connections to your little sister . . . well, this child would be one I knew you would search for with a drive that would surpass all your other 'salvages.'"

The panic I'd been feeling was now full blown and I struggled, unable to stop my body from trying to escape a fate I knew would somehow be worse than if he was just going to kill me. He'd set me up, he'd done all this to get me here. I continued to push my panic into the beast holding me.

The air around us stilled, it grew heavy, and then the shit hit the proverbial fan.

The beast let out a mind-numbing roar, flinging its hands off me and, in doing so, sent the cloaked man tumbling through the air. My feet slid to the ground and I sprinted toward the stairs. I could only hope he hadn't locked down both of the entrances.

Heavy thuds resounded behind me, a screech shook the castle foundations, and then silence for a split second.

"RYLEE!" His voice struck a chord through to my bones. My feet stuttered, and I slowed.

I needed help, badly. Reaching out, I tapped into the person who'd stepped between me and the cloaked man before.

"O'Shea." I whimpered, and locked onto his emotions. The intensity of his feelings stung me, sharper than any child's would ever be. Fear overridden by true concern, focus, wanting to do the right thing. I held onto him like I would a life raft in rough seas and started to run again. The stairs blurred by. I passed the initiation room and found myself in the hallway where I could see the doorway.

Heart firing like a jackrabbit on speed, I fumbled at the handle, and it was the split second mistake he needed to catch up to me, pinning me to the door with his body.

"You were just going to run out on me?" His voice was no longer a soft seduction, but a deadly ice that made my mouth dry.

"You seemed busy," I said, unable to turn off my bitch switch. He tried to flip me around to face him, but I fought even that. I was so close to escape. Suddenly, I knew how the children being snatched must have felt. He handled me as if I was a child, his movements sure and steady as I flailed, using every trick I knew in an attempt to escape, knowing all along I couldn't fight him forever. He just had to wait me out. Screaming, I knew I was losing, his deceiving calm holding back the anger brewing beneath the façade. All my training, all the strength I'd built on over the years, was nothing to him.

"Fuck!" I knew he almost had me. I could feel my resistance to him slowing. For all I was worth, I clung to O'Shea's emotions.

"Let go of him."

"No."

"Do as I say, Rylee." His words were so insistent; I wanted to do as he asked. I wanted to please him.

My body shivered, caught between the two men. I had nothing left to fight, and his lips covered mine, his tongue plunging into the depths of my mouth. Power flowed between us, and he ground his hips into mine, his desire obvious. I wasn't Milly, but I knew an out when one was given to me. Still hanging onto O'Shea's emotions, I kissed the cloaked man back until his arms went around me, sliding down over my hips, cupping my ass against his ever hardening body.

His hands started to strip me out of my clothes and at that moment, I sensed his loss of control. He couldn't fuck me and keep a handle on my psyche at the same time. Still, I kept my eyes closed. I didn't want to see his eyes, those icy blue eyes that sucked me in like some sort of vortex. I had a feeling if I looked him in the face, no amount of control lost on his part would save me.

Instead, I started to strip the cloak off him, pulling it over his head, and the horny fool let me. Like a hockey player starting a fight, I lifted the cloak up, got it halfway over his head, tangled it, and shoved him backwards, kicking out at his left knee. The joint gave way under my foot, and he screamed. Thank you, Doran, for that little gem.

I spun, yanked the door open, and tumbled through into the caves. Without a goddamned light. All the Coven members were dead, so all of their Witchlights were out.

In the pitch black, I was unable to see my hand, let alone know where I was going. But, I had a plan. In a manner of speaking.

The plan was to follow along the edge of the wall until I hit the bodies of the two witches we'd killed. If the woman was still alive she could make a Witchlight; if she wasn't, surely one of them would have something on them I could use. Surely.

Of course, three steps in and the door behind me opened. The man—sorcerer—whatever the fuck he was, was right behind me. With a light. Well, that would work. I bolted down the cavern with him right on my tail. Even with his busted leg, he was *fast*. The upside was he was no longer trying to control me. The downside was that I knew if he wasn't trying to control me, he was going to try and kill me.

Arms pumping, sweat dripping down the side of my face, I could taste the dusty cavern on the back of my tongue with each desperate breath I took. Fingers grazed the back of my jeans giving me an extra spurt of adrenaline.

We raced through the cavern and turned a corner that turned into a near spill for me. As I looked up from my scramble, I could see the harness dangling, like manna from heaven.

Three feet away, I leapt for it and started to climb, but he was too close and latched onto my ankle before I could get out of reach.

"We're not done yet, Rylee."

I didn't answer, and just kicked out with my free foot, catching him in the forehead, snapping his head back. A flash of white fangs and those icy blue eyes made me scream.

Vampire, he was a vampire.

The rope was nearly yanked out of my hands as someone began to haul me up. I fought my urge to flee and the urge to drop back to the ground to try to finish him off. Berget, my Berget, had been taken by vampires.

Self preservation kicked in and I clung to the rope as it—and I—were pulled to the surface. Hanging from the rope, I had time to think, time to ponder. But I did nothing. I let my mind go blank, let my fear hold me onto the rope for the lifeline it was. I was yanked from the mineshaft and slapped into handcuffs. My Miranda rights read to me. My mind numb. I was unable to believe what had just happened, and I didn't fight them.

From below, the vampire called up to me. "I'm not what you think I am, Rylee. But not to worry, we'll meet again. I promise you that."

For the first time in my life, I was grateful for the police. Of course, at that particular moment they were arresting me for multiple murders of FBI agents, not to mention I was in league with the rogue former FBI Agent O'Shea, and being accused of being the leader of a kidnapping ring. The moon had risen since we'd been in the mineshaft, the soft light picked up the blood more effectively than if we saw it under the bright light of the day. Even to me, it seemed surreal, and I was used to the weird and supernatural side of the world.

They shoved me into an armored transport vehicle, two FBI agents in with me, their guns visible and their hatred of me, a cop killer in their eyes, obvious. I didn't care. At that point, all I wanted was to sleep, and I knew a jail would be as safe, or safer, than any place I could find. The one bright side was that I knew O'Shea and Milly would get the two kids to safety, and with that thought tumbling through my mind, I leaned my head back and closed my eyes.

26

Getting the kids to the hospital was the first priority; a close second was getting Adamson back to the human side of whatever the hell she'd crossed over.

O'Shea drove, careening into the hospital parking lot, all the while wondering at why Milly had insisted they leave. Once India was settled and Jake was rushed off into the emergency room, the witch grabbed him by the arm and dragged him outside, finally answering the question he'd asked what felt like a hundred times on the drive to the hospital.

"You don't get it, Agent; we can't get her back from that route, we have to go to where the two of you came in. If it's still open, she has a chance." Her eyes flashed bright green at him.

He nodded. "Okay, but then we're going to have to hurry."

A shuffle behind them, one of the nurses that had admitted the kids, cleared her throat. "Excuse me, are you Agent O'Shea?"

Surprised, he started to say yes, but thought about the belief that he was a cop killer, and the word froze on his lips.

He needn't have worried, the witch ratted him out.

"Yes, he is," she said.

"There's a phone call, urgent. Agent Valley, he said his name was." She beckoned them inside.

O'Shea's surprise turned to shock. Valley was second in the bureau only to Jessop Darlington. O'Shea took a breath, knowing the phone call was either going to be very good, or very, very bad.

He just didn't know which one.

Jail wasn't so bad. Not if you overlooked the smell of urine and vomit under the pine-scented cleaner that had been used. I was in my own cell, a single hard bed with no mattress, a toilet, and a sink. Of course, it wasn't a jail, not really. I was in the holding cells below the Bismarck police department. I had a couple of neighbors, but they were both sleeping off the party from the night before by the sounds of it, though I suspected they'd added to the smell I couldn't get away from. Pacing, I mulled over my options.

Sleep hadn't come as easy as I'd hoped. My mind had been unable to let go of the fear and inability to fight back that man, vampire, whatever he was. Then there was O'Shea. I kept checking in with him, and the emotions were freaking me out a bit. Surprise, pleasure, happiness. Had he slept with Milly? It wouldn't surprise me, not when it came to my best friend. But then, why was there a sudden stab of anger that rode shotgun to that thought?

Nope, not going there.

Footsteps sounded down the long hallway that was the only way in or out. My heart clenched; what if it was the vampire? There was no way I could get away from him, not here. It was the middle of the night and totally plausible that he could walk right in and snatch me.

Two black suits came into view, mirrored glasses and an almost comical resemblance to *Men in Black*.

"So, which one of you was played by Will Smith?" I leaned a hip against the bars. "I mean, you're both white, so . . ." I lifted an eyebrow at them.

"You need to come with us, Ma'am." They opened the door, cuffed me, and escorted me down the long hallway, up the stairs and out the front door into a waiting black van. Just like the ones that had been chasing us. The Arcane Division was not something I wanted anything to do with. I hadn't even had a chance to read through the papers I had on them yet.

Slumping backwards, I leaned against their hands. "I think I'd rather stay in jail, to be honest; black vans and I just don't look good together."

They said nothing, just picked me up, opened the door, and tossed me in. The back of the van was dark, only splashes of light from the street lamps peeked in through cracks near the back door. They drove for close to three hours, long enough to get us well out of town, long enough for me to slip the cuffs from back to front and try the door multiple times.

When the door slid open I launched myself out into the early morning sun, the wind whipping my hair around my face, blurring my vision for a split second. I stumbled to a stop. We were at my house.

"Inside. Move."

Now, thoroughly confused, I did as I was told.

Stepping lightly, I climbed the steps. The front door was slightly ajar, so I pushed it with my shoulder and peeked in. Sitting in my living room was O'Shea, Milly, and a man in a suit who had to be FBI by his posture alone, but I didn't recognize him. Older, he had streaks of grey in his light brown hair. Brown eyes that looked as though they might have flecks of green in them were his best feature. His face was jowly, nose offset, and it looked as though he had an overbite. But there was an air of confidence that made me think he was in charge.

The stranger stood. "Ms. Adamson. My name is Agent Valley." He motioned at my handcuffs. "Here, let me take those off for you."

O'Shea stood. "No, I've got it." He stepped over to me and I tried not to look him in the face, tried not to think about him and Milly in bed together. She always did move fast. He unlocked the cuffs, his fingers lingering for split second on my wrists.

Ignoring the others, I asked him the only question that really mattered to me. "Did the kids make it out okay?"

He smiled, really smiled, and I hated how my heart tried to flop about in my chest like a fucking Labrador retriever whose best friend just showed up.

"India is back with her parents, though I think you need to speak with them still. And Jake is in intensive care, but it looks like he'll pull through."

Relief swept through me. Two kids were back where they belonged. Now I could finally shift gears and deal with the rest of my crazy life.

"Please have a seat, we have a lot to discuss," Agent Valley said.

Frowning, unable to even guess at what was about to happen, I shook my head. "No, I'll stand."

He shrugged. "Fine, fine. You've been exonerated of any charges relating to the deaths of the Agents at the mineshaft."

"Why? How?"

Valley shrugged. "We know it was a Harpy. Nothing to do about that but post men to keep people away from the beast."

Shock rippled through me; my jaw dropped and I shut it with an audible click. "But . . . what . . . how?"

"We are a part of the Arcane Division of the FBI, Ms. Adamson. We know a great deal about the supernatural and we're doing our best to manage the interactions between them and humans. It doesn't always go well." He barked out a dry, humorless laugh. "As I suppose you already know from your own experiences with the law."

"Okay," I said. "Fine, you know about us. Good for you. What does that have to do with me?"

Valley nodded to O'Shea. "Liam here has also been exonerated, though he can't go back to the division he was in. Even though we have a plausible cover story, we can't convince all the other Agents that the death of one of their own, by one of their own, was acceptable."

Both of my eyebrows shot into my hairline and before I could ask, O'Shea explained.

"The story is that Martins was in on the child-kidnapping ring and that he shot at me first. Of course, it doesn't hurt that I showed up at a hospital with two of the missing children and the bodies of two others."

Valley leaned back in my favorite chair and stretched his legs out in front of him; short as they were, they didn't even reach the coffee table a mere two feet away. "We've pulled Liam into our division. But" —he raised a finger— "he needs a partner. Someone who is savvy to the ways of the supernatural elements of this world, someone who can help him, and in turn help us."

I folded my arms across my chest, the tightening of bonds and responsibilities I didn't want creeping in around me. "And if I don't agree to this?"

The senior agent shrugged. "Nothing. This is not blackmail. We need you. You'd be on payroll of course, and would have access to all of our training facilities, weapons, and any equipment you'd need."

"Could I still go after my own cases?"

He shook his head. "No, anyone who comes to you would then be put through the system. Of course, you'd still be bringing children, people home."

Licking my lips, I looked to Milly. She shrugged ever so slightly. "I need to think about it."

Valley agreed, stood, and handed me his card. "Call me when you're ready to do the right thing."

I had to hold back an urge to strike out at him for poking at my weak spot. Guilt was the one thing I couldn't escape, the one thing that drove me more than any other, and of course, those shrewd eyes that had a moment ago seemed kind, saw that in me.

Valley left, but O'Shea stayed behind. Milly stood, touched the agent on the shoulder and said, "Call me."

He nodded, his eyes tracking her as she left the room. I didn't have any right to feel upset. Milly always got the guy. It was nothing new. Ignoring my traitorous emotions, I faced O'Shea.

"What about your partner, Martins? Will his name be blacklisted?" It was stupid to ask, but I wasn't sure what else to say. How could I be his partner? It wouldn't work. We were too different.

"His family will get a sizeable payout, and his funeral will be all paid for. No expense spared. It was the best they could do. Until the government decides to let the general populace know, it's the best we could come up with." His shoulders sagged. "I want you . . ."

My breath caught.

". . . as my partner." His dark eyes lifted to mine. "But I'd understand if you turned it down."

Nodding, I said nothing, for once somewhat speechless. I wanted to go back to the days where I felt nothing for this human standing in front of me. Nothing but contempt, anger, maybe even hatred. Simple to feel those things, not so simple to start caring.

"I'll let you know."

He nodded and brushed past me, the scent of his cologne and the mint I remembered from his lips catching me off guard, making me sway on my feet.

The room was silent, but for the steady breathing that was my attempt to calm the confusion rushing through me.

A sniffle at the door caught my ear. I lifted my hand, not needing to turn around. "Alex." There was the scrabble of feet on the rough wooden floor, and then a large furry body wrapped around my legs and helped to ground me. I crouched down and hugged him; buried my face into his neck.

"Rylee sad," he grumbled, his arms awkwardly circling me.

"A little. But I'll be okay."

"Harpy sad too."

I'd forgotten about that little detail. I stood, brushed my face off as though I wasn't crying and strode to the door. "Where is she roosting, Alex?"

He bolted out the door and I trotted after him. He made a beeline for the half-rotted barn. Pushing the door open, I stepped into the mote-filled air. The light streamed through the broken slats and gave a picturesque scene, if not for the Harpy dozing in the old hay.

"Eve?" I didn't step any further into the room. As it was, I could leap out and slam the door if I had too. Alex, though, had no qualms. He trotted forward and stuck his nose under her chin. "Evie."

She fluttered awake, her eyes blinking slowly. "Hello, Tracker."

"You can call me, Rylee," I said, my hands itching for a weapon, even though she had claimed sanctuary with me. Harpy's were not trusted for a reason.

"Rylee, then. I chased away the pack that was here; it didn't take much."

That explained that. Maybe having a Harpy around wouldn't be all bad. I nodded my thanks. Alex, though, didn't hold back, almost throwing himself at the young Harpy; she brushed him off, but not in an unkind way.

"What are you going to do?" Her voice was devoid of any emotion.

It hit me that she was depressed, which made sense. I'd lost my sister, I knew what it was to lose a beloved sibling and think you should have somehow saved them.

Breathing in the scent of hay and years of dust, I made my way over to her, sat down, and talked. About Berget, about my life, about how I wanted to save those kids who got snatched. Her eyes went wide as I opened up to her like I'd only ever done with Milly, and Eve seemed to sense it.

"Why are you telling me all of this?"

By now Alex was laying across my lap.

"Because I know what it is to be lost, to want to find your own path, one that can maybe redeem the past," I said, my voice thick with sorrow even to my own ears.

She nodded slowly as she took it all in. "May I help you? Would you let me?"

That was not expected, and it was my turn to nod slowly. "Yes, you could help me. But I have to ask, Eve, how can you be so accepting of me? I killed both of your sisters."

Her feathers fluffed up. "In our culture, it is the strong who survive, the strong who are revered. You were able to kill my sisters; they were not strong enough. You outsmarted them. I would learn from you so that I do not follow in their footsteps. It is often our way to train with those who have killed our family members."

Wow. Shock filtered through me. That was not what I expected, not at all. "Okay, you have strengths I could only ever hope for to tap into when searching for kids, but don't you want to go to your own kind?"

Eve snorted and fluffed her body. "They kicked us out because we . . . no, I cannot speak of it yet. They don't like me, or my sisters." Her throat caught, and I placed a hand, gingerly, on her wing, feeling the tremble of emotion ripple through her body. It seemed I was bound to pick up strays and outcasts.

Leaving her there, I went back inside the house, passed on my usual routine for the first time in years, showered, went to bed and lay there staring up at the ceiling, Alex stretched out across my legs. Thoughts of O'Shea, Milly, Eve, Alex, India, and Giselle ran through my mind until, finally exhausted, I fell asleep, hoping the morning light would give me some guidance as to what would happen next.

27

A week later, India and her parents met me at the hotel where I'd first met them. While Maria and Don were grateful, they were reserved. India had no such qualms.

I stepped into the room and she ran toward me, arms outstretched. Scooping her up, I held her tight. Today, she smelled only like baby powder, no scent of blood.

"How are you feeling, kid?" I put her back down and crouched so we were eye to eye. I rubbed at the spot on my body where the demon's scorpion tail had pierced my prone form in the pentagram. Nothing seemed to have come from it, but there was a dull ache that wouldn't go away. It was particularly bad at night. For now though, I'd ignore it. If it ain't broke, don't fix it and all that jazz.

"Okay. I like Danny." Danny was the therapist I'd set them up with. She also happened to be a true psychic who would be able to help India train her abilities.

"That's good. She's a nice lady."

We visited for a few more minutes before I headed toward the door. India grabbed my hand, pulling me down to her level. "I have to tell you something."

Smiling, I tipped my head so she could whisper into my ear.

"Berget says that Giselle is the key to finding her."

Her words, so simple, set me back on my heels, and I had to kneel down to catch my breath. "How?"

India shrugged, keeping her voice low. A look over her shoulder, she waved off her parents, who had tensed at my apparent shock. "I can see them, the spirits. Your sister, she stayed with me. Told me things. She said that it wasn't your fault. That she's too far away for you to find. But—" India twisted her hands around mine. "Berget says that Giselle can help you find her."

"That doesn't make any sense," I whispered.

She shrugged. "It's what she told me. Will you still look for her?"

I nodded. "I've never stopped."

"That's what I told her too." India wrapped her arms around my neck. "I told her that you would always come for the missing children. Everyone knows that."

A lump formed hard in my throat, one that I couldn't swallow past. India made me swear I'd stay in touch. I could barely nod, and struggled to get out to my Jeep, where I laid my head on the steering wheel and finally let the tears flow.

Berget was still out there, and she didn't blame me for not finding her. It took me a long time to pull myself together, but for the first time I felt . . . free of the guilt.

Jake pulled through, though he was going to be in a wheelchair for a while; both of his legs had been broken and quite badly, but he was alive and had no memory of what had happened to him. I visited him in the hospital, only once, and while he was sleeping. He wouldn't remember me anyway. From what the nurses told me, he already wanted to be just like his new hero, Agent O'Shea. Jake wanted to be an FBI Agent when he grew up. Boo-yah.

Milly moved out of the Coven and in with me, Alex and Giselle, who'd come to live with us until we knew what would be best for her. I was happy, yet I had no desire to hear Milly and O'Shea 'knocking boots' in the room across from me, so I implemented a 'No Sex at the House' rule, which she seemed to be fine with.

Two weeks after Agent Valley visited me, I got a phone call from him. I didn't answer. I still wasn't ready to face that particular choice yet. Worse yet, the stack of papers on the Arcane division of the FBI had gone missing; most likely it got grabbed in one or the other raids on my place, so I had no further knowledge than what Valley was willing to give me, which wasn't enough to sway me.

All and all, life went back to as normal as it could, at least for me.

That is, until the phone rang and Dox's voice came through on the other end, his voice heavy with sorrow, his words telling me my time off was up.

"Rylee, we've got a problem."

COMING HOLIDAY 2016 FROM TALOS PRESS

IMMUNE

A Rylee Adamson Novel
Book 2

"My name is Rylee, and I am a Tracker."

When children go missing, and the Humans have no leads, I'm the one they call. I am their last hope in bringing home the lost ones. I salvage what they cannot.

Underestimating demons is a bad idea, and it's a mistake that may cost me not only my own life, but the life of a missing child.

If I can swallow my pride, and allow Agent O'Shea to help me find a way to deal with the demon, we might be able to save the child.

With this salvage, it's a race against time, a test of trust, and a temptation that I'm doing my damnedest to ignore.

If only swallowing my pride was that easy.

Starring the irresistible, ass-kicking heroine Rylee Adamson, *Immune* is the second book in *USA Today* bestselling author Shannon Mayer's sexy, exciting, and laugh-out-loud series, a dangerously addictive paranormal romance.

$7.99 mass market paperback
978-1-940456-96-6

AN EXCERPT FROM IMMUNE

"**A**lex, get back on your side!"

He did as I asked, though he continued to bounce in his seat, actually rocking the Jeep from side to side. His breath fogged up the windows something fierce.

I cracked my window and said, "Roll down your window, Alex."

"Snow, snow, snow, snow!" He chanted, not bothering to keep his volume down as he scrambled with his window, rolling it halfway down, a blast of cold air filling the Jeep.

Unfortunately, he was bang on. The white stuff had been falling steadily for over three hours and the road crews seemed to be taking the day off. There was a thin goat trail for vehicles where there should have been two full lanes. The other side of the highway didn't look any better. We should have been into Bismarck already, but we were maybe halfway at best. Shit, I was going to miss my appointment.

Windshield wipers on high, the snow was so heavy it was like driving through a swirling fog, and I leaned forward to get a better view. Middle of the day, lights on, and I still couldn't see where the hell I was going. Not a good start to this little trip.

The wind blew hard, throwing the Jeep sideways. Fighting the steering wheel, I cursed under my breath. Immune, I might be, unable to be turned into anything furry or blood sucking, and a Tracker of children using my innate abilities. But, I could still be killed. And driving in bad weather like this was not one of my talents. It was the only downside to living where I did, in my opinion.

"Come on," I grumbled at the weather. Anger was easier to hang onto than fear. Better in this case, 'cause being afraid would only give me more trouble.

"Come on," Alex grumbled, shaking a fist at the windshield. Shit, that werewolf made me laugh. I hated to admit he was one of the best things that had ever wandered into my life.

And what about O'Shea? Well, I didn't think stalking me for ten years counted as 'wandering into my life.'

Besides, he'd been hanging with Milly; they were lovers, while he and I were . . . what the hell were we? Not friends, not enemies, something in between. Fifty shades of grey, my ass; there were at least a thousand, if you asked me.

My heater took that moment to kick off and within moments the cab filled with icy cold air. Alex didn't mind, his thick coat perfectly suited to the weather, but a sharp pang in my chest shot through me. I tried to draw a breath, struggled to get a gulp of the cold air. What was happening? I took my foot off the gas pedal, let the Jeep start to slow down on its own as

I fought the now crushing pain in the middle of my chest. Each breath I took rattled in my throat, as if I were sucking in water as well as air. Hands clenching the steering wheel, I tried to pull over, but my muscles wouldn't respond, my foot not even reacting when I made an attempt to lift if off the gas pedal. A flicker of an image danced in front of the Jeep.

The last salvage I'd completed involved a demon. We'd fought, I'd beaten it with a little help from my friends, but it had nailed me with its stinger before dying. The demon's antennae twitched in the wind, its black body standing out in the white snow. Shaped like an ant standing upright with a scorpion tail arcing over its head, I knew the thing could fight, but we'd sent it back to where it'd come from. Hadn't we? Shit, I thought we'd killed it. Maybe not.

The demon faded out from in front of the Jeep and I let out a breath, forcing the air from my lungs. I must have been seeing things, my eyes playing tricks on me. Like an asthma attack, I struggled for each breath, but pushed on driving. If I stopped here, there was a good chance we'd not be found until morning and if the temperatures dropped, well, let's just say I had no intention of being a Popsicle anytime soon.

Alex started to bark, a high-pitched sharp, fear-filled staccato that burst through the fog of whatever was happening to me.

"Rylee, Rylee, Rylee!"

I opened my eyes, unaware I'd even closed them. Right in front of us was a grader, horn blowing as I drove straight toward it.

I yanked the steering wheel hard to the left. The Jeep slewed around the larger vehicle and into the deep snow on the side of the road.

"Fuck!"

The edge of the road disappeared into whiteness when the Jeep hit something hard, snapping it up, flipping us ass over tea kettle. The world seemed to go still as we floated for a brief moment, and I fought to stay conscious.

We landed hard, but the snow partially cushioned us—the only good thing to happen so far. Groaning, I hung upside down in my seatbelt, the material digging into my chest, increasing the pressure on my sternum, driving me to the brink of blacking out. The cold filled me, but didn't numb me. Cold fire raced through my veins, my body spasmed.

Alex whimpered, licked my hand, but I couldn't stop the tremors. I had no control over my own body. Only my eyes would do as I commanded and that didn't exactly help. The windshield was caved in and I stared at the white snow, again the image of the demon dancing in front of me. Laughing.

"Bastard." I coughed and spit at the snow. Blood flecked the white, my lip split from hitting the steering wheel.

"Alex, go," I said, my voice a bare whisper.

"No, stay with Rylee," He leaned forward to put his face close to mine, balancing on the steering wheel and hitting the horn before settling off to one side. I wanted to cover my ears, but couldn't even lift my hands. Was I paralyzed? Now that would seriously screw up my life.

Dark spots and bright lights swirled in my vision. In desperation I reached out with my abilities to the one person I knew I could hang onto.

Tracking O'Shea was easy, his mind an open book to me. And he was a hell of a lot closer than I'd expected.

He was close enough that his emotions were right inside my head, less than a hundred feet away. Confusion, anger, and worry were at the front of the line and they swamped me with their intensity. Pulling back from him, I tried to lift my hand, to no avail. "Alex. Horn. Hit it."

Alex reared up and jammed both front paws onto the horn, the sound jarring my senses. Nausea rolled over me and vertigo hit me hard, made me want to throw up.

The dark of unconsciousness swallowed me whole between one breath and the next. Distantly, I could feel hands on my body, a voice I knew speaking softly to me. But what I was seeing inside the darkness held my attention.

I'd met this one before, on the other side of the Veil, after we'd rescued India. He stood watching me, an eyebrow quirked up into his hairline. Crystal clear blue eyes regarded me. "You have yet to even ask my name."

I frowned. "I don't care what your name is."

He smiled. "You may call me Faris. Will you speak with me?"

The darkness seemed to shift around us, putting me only a few feet away from him. I tensed, confused by the feeling of hands on me while I could see that he hadn't touched me. "I think I'll pass." The thing was,

I couldn't turn away from him; my body still wasn't obeying me.

He tipped his head to one side and stepped closer to me. "The demon that struck you was a Hoarfrost demon. It is designed to turn its carrier into an epicenter for a new ice age. Of course, that only works if the venom can be assimilated. Not the case with you. However, it is slowing you down. Until you deal with it, the cold will follow you, make you vulnerable to all sorts of nasty things." He leaned closer, his breath brushing across my cheek.

Panic clawed at me. "No, I'm an Immune. I can't be killed by venom."

"I didn't say it would kill you, not the venom at least. But it's hurting you nonetheless, and the side effects of it, they could kill you. You aren't immune to hypothermia. It makes you vulnerable, unable to defend yourself. I quite like the change in you." He lifted a hand and brushed it across my cheek, then down to my bottom lip, tugging at it.

I jerked my head away, the only part of me I seemed to have control over. "Why would you tell me this?"

"I want us to be friends."

Laughing, I threw my head back. "That's why you tried to kill me?"

Faris smiled at me, a glimpse of fangs coyly peeking out from beneath thin lips. "You'd upset me. I hadn't expected you to turn from me as you did. Do you know how long it's been since I've had a woman turn me down?"

"Obviously not long enough."

Ghost hands slid over my skin and I shivered recognizing O'Shea's touch. Then those hands that were being so gentle slapped my face, snapping my head to one side.

Faris laughed. "I will tell you one thing because I want you to trust me. There is a way to purge the demon venom. Ask Doran, he will explain. Until then, try to stay warm. Or you could wait for it to run its course, hiding somewhere the snow never flies. That might take a few years." He lifted his hand, fingertips brushing lightly along my jaw line. "Even Immunes can be hurt, Rylee. Remember that."

He gave me a slow smile and I glared at him. Not exactly an effective deterrent.

"Perhaps we will speak another time." He was suddenly holding me tight, his lips above mine, fangs extended. Panic clawed at me; I couldn't fight, couldn't even begin to push him away.

I screamed, pushing all my energy toward shoving him away, and a bright light burst beside us. It was his turn to scream, fleeing from the bright pulsing light as I crumpled to the ground.

Hands caught me, a face I saw only in my dreams hovering over me.

"Berget," I whispered. She smiled down at me, blue eyes sparkling with love and laughter.

"Rylee, be careful. Faris wants you badly, and he will do anything to gain your trust. This one time, though, he is right. Go to Doran."

This was not like the dreams I had with her in them. This was real; she was here with me.

"I can't find you," I said, tears choking me. "I keep trying but . . ."

She shushed me. "I know. I don't blame you. This is no one's fault. This is destiny. You will understand in time." Leaning over me, she kissed me on the forehead and I opened my eyes to see O'Shea leaning over me.

"Adamson!"

I managed a weak, "Hey." Then I promptly closed my eyes. I wasn't out of it, I just couldn't look at his face, see the worry and concern there. I didn't want to feel anything right now. My emotions were a jumble of my own and O'Shea's, and I was struggling to separate them. What had happened when I blacked out? Had I really spoken with Berget? Was she alive somewhere? Was Faris really able to contact me when I was unconscious? That would not be good.

A cold, wet nose jammed into my ear.

"Alex scared."

O'Shea lifted me up like I was nothing, cradling me against his chest. The world tilted as he walked, and I could hear sirens in the distance.

"We have to go," I mumbled. "I'm okay, I just need to warm up."

O'Shea didn't stop moving. "You were in a car accident, you are not okay."

"Not the accident. The demon. From before." Hating that Faris was the one to cue me into my problem, I could now feel the venom pumping through my system. It was slowing everything down, making it hard for me to keep breathing. There had to be a way to get it out of me, but I didn't want to believe Doran was my only hope. Milly didn't deal with demons; she wouldn't know what to do anymore than I did. Shit, I didn't want to believe Faris, to trust he was telling me the truth, but it wasn't looking like I had any choice.

O'Shea's arms tightened around me, then relaxed as he slid me into the back seat of his SUV. I tried to sit up.

"Lay down. Alex, here, get in beside her." A damp, but warm body pressed up against mine, his head resting on my legs.

I forced my eyes open. "I need to get warm, the venom . . ."

That was it, my strength was done.

ABOUT THE AUTHOR

Shannon Mayer is the *USA Today* bestselling author of the Rylee Adamson novels, the Elemental series, and numerous paranormal romance, urban fantasy, mystery, and suspense novels. She lives in the southwestern tip of Canada with her husband, son, and numerous other animals.